"I quit."

Amy winced, feeling suddenly emotional. She loved this job. She'd even come pretty close to loving her boss a time or two. But if she was going to have any sort of life at all, she was going to have to leave this all behind. "I—I'm afraid I'm not going to be able to work here anymore."

Carter gave her a long-suffering look. "What do you want, Pendleton? A raise? A new title? More responsibility?"

"I want..." She hesitated. She'd never really told him this before, though she'd hinted at it often enough lately. "I want a home. I want a husband. I want babies, and a cat, and long mornings in bed and walks on the beach."

"What?"

Dear Reader,

Summer's finally here! Whether you'll be lounging poolside, at the beach, or simply in your home this season, we have great reads packed with everything you enjoy from Silhouette Romance—tenderness, emotion, fun and, of course, heart-pounding romance—plus some very special surprises.

First, don't miss the exciting conclusion to the thrilling ROYALLY WED: THE MISSING HEIR miniseries with Cathie Linz's *A Prince at Last!* Then be swept off your feet—just like the heroine herself!—in Hayley Gardner's *Kidnapping His Bride.*

Romance favorite Raye Morgan is back with *A Little Moonlighting,* about a tycoon set way off track by his beguiling associate who wants a family to call her own. And in Debrah Morris's *That Maddening Man,* can a traffic-stopping smile convince a career woman—and single mom—to slow down…?

Then laugh, cry and fall in love all over again with two incredibly tender love stories. Vivienne Wallington's *Kindergarten Cupids* is a very different, highly emotional story about scandal, survival and second chances. Then dive right into Jackie Braun's *True Love, Inc.,* about a professional matchmaker who's challenged to find her very sexy, very cynical client his perfect woman. Can she convince him that she already has?

Here's to a wonderful, relaxing summer filled with happiness and romance. See you next month with more fun-in-the-sun selections.

Happy reading!

Mary-Theresa Hussey

Mary-Theresa Hussey
Senior Editor

Please address questions and book requests to:
Silhouette Reader Service
U.S.: 3010 Walden Ave., P.O. Box 1325, Buffalo, NY 14269
Canadian: P.O. Box 609, Fort Erie, Ont. L2A 5X3

A Little Moonlighting

RAYE MORGAN

SILHOUETTE *Romance*®

Published by Silhouette Books

America's Publisher of Contemporary Romance

This one is for Val Payne,
good friend and fellow water polo mom

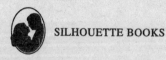 SILHOUETTE BOOKS

ISBN 0-373-19595-8

A LITTLE MOONLIGHTING

This edition published by arrangement with Harlequin Books S.A.

® and TM are trademarks of Harlequin Books S.A., used under license.
Trademarks indicated with ® are registered in the United States Patent
and Trademark Office, the Canadian Trade Marks Office and in other
countries.

Visit Silhouette at www.eHarlequin.com

Printed in U.S.A.

Books by Raye Morgan

RAYE MORGAN

has spent almost two decades, while writing over fifty novels, searching for the answer to that elusive question: Just what is that special magic that happens when a man and a woman fall in love? Every time she thinks she has the answer, a new wrinkle pops up, necessitating another book! Meanwhile, after living in Holland, Guam, Japan and Washington, D.C., she currently makes her home in Southern California with her husband and two of her four boys.

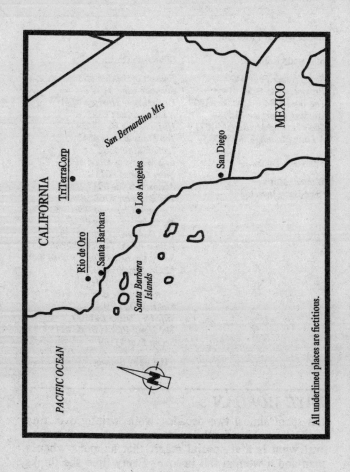

CALIFORNIA

PACIFIC OCEAN

Rio de Oro

Santa Barbara

TriTerraCorp

San Bernardino Mts

Los Angeles

Santa Barbara Islands

San Diego

MEXICO

N

All underlined places are fictitious.

Chapter One

"Pack your bags, Pendleton. We'll be dining in Paris tomorrow."

Amy Pendleton looked up from her desk with a worried frown, her sleek blond head tilted to the side as she regarded her boss, Carter James, who seemed all too cheerful with his news.

"Paris, France?" she asked, a slight hint of desperation in her tone.

"Of course," he replied, waving papers at her before he dropped them on her desktop. His clear blue eyes shone with anticipation. "Ah, the Seine, the Champs-Élysées, the streetside bistros…"

Her pretty face twisted as her brows pulled together. "Weren't we just in Paris last month?" she asked, wondering why he never seemed to notice that her enthusiasm for these constant business trips had waned in recent months. "Or was that Amsterdam?"

"Both," he said happily, dropping to sit on the corner of her desk, one leg swinging. "And don't forget that great steak dinner we had in Madrid on that trip. Too bad the meeting in Copenhagen lasted so late into the night that we had to settle for herring sandwiches."

"Herring sandwiches," she echoed, her voice hollow, her eyes glazed over. Absently, she picked up a pencil and held it in her hands. "Another cross-Atlantic flight. Cardboard airplane food." She snapped the pencil in two and let the pieces drop onto her desk as she stared into a grim future. "Hour-long waits at ticket counters." She picked up another pencil and snapped it, too. "Wearing clothes so wrinkled they look as though you'd slept in them." Snap went a third. "No sleep. Jet lag. No way to keep track of the days."

A deep sigh shuddered through her. "I just want to spend three consecutive nights in my own bed," she said wistfully.

"Remember that little café where we had that great Turkish coffee the last time we were in Paris?" Carter said, his eyes focused on a distant memory.

His handsome face was relaxed, content. The picture of the successful businessman, his wide shoulders filled out his impeccable Italian suit as though he'd been born to wear the style. His thick dark hair was combed back in a slight wave off his forehead, but perfectly controlled, as was most of his life. "We'll go there for breakfast on our first morning…"

She stared at him. He wasn't paying any attention. But that was hardly new. He never paid any attention to her! Another pencil bit the dust.

How had she ever been so crazy as to dream about someday marrying this man when, after two long years of working together, he barely knew she existed outside of her performance as his administrative associate? He went on, rhapsodizing about Paris in the spring, and she marveled at him. How could he be so absolutely adorable and at the same time, so darn self-involved?

Marry him? Ha. Now *that* would be the height of insanity. First she would have to get him to think about something other than business or food long enough to notice she was a woman. And that seemed to be asking a little too much.

Although, she'd tried. Oh, yes, she'd certainly tried. She'd done all the normal things—brought in home-baked brownies, laughed at his jokes, smiled a lot, sat around looking doe-eyed and feminine.

And when that didn't seem to jolt a response in him, she'd tried a more direct approach. She'd asked for advice from friends and—much to her later chagrin—had taken it. The short skirts hadn't done anything noticeable to stir his blood. But she'd pressed on, donning dresses that emphasized her attributes, wearing her hair loose and casually shaking it in his face when she bent close to look over plans he was explaining to her.

"Pendleton, you're going to make me sneeze," he'd said, grimacing. "Can't you do something with that hair?"

She remembered well the incident when she'd tried out the new perfume her friend Julie had told her was a surefire attention-getter. She'd stood very close to Carter and wafted the scent around her in his general direction whenever she got the chance. And suddenly, it seemed to work. He was sniffing the air.

"What's that smell?" he asked her, frowning.

But before she could answer, while she was still busy producing her most flirtatious smile, he decided he knew.

"Someone's ordered in pizza," he said decisively. "My God, I'm hungry as a bear. Hold down the fort, Pendleton. I'll go get us something to eat."

Being mistaken for a freshly baked pizza was something a girl just didn't get over all that quickly. That had been the last straw. She'd pretty much given up now.

And here he was going on and on about Paris as though this trip was going to be something special. Well, not for her.

"I'm not going," she announced when he paused for breath.

He looked at her as though he wasn't sure he'd heard right. "What are you talking about?" But before she could answer, he noticed the shattered remains littering her desk. "Pendleton, why are you destroying your pencils?"

She glared at him. "Because I am slowly going mad," she told him grimly. "And that is why I am going to quit."

She pulled open a desk drawer with a flourish and took out a sheet of paper that had her resignation printed on it. She'd been holding it there for weeks, waiting for the right moment. That moment seemed to have come.

"Here. Take it. I think it covers all the bases." She winced, feeling suddenly emotional. She loved this job. She'd even come pretty close to loving her boss a time or two. But if she was going to have any sort of life at all, she was going to have to leave this all behind. "I—I'm afraid I'm not going to be able to work here anymore."

He glanced at the paper, read a line or two, and gave her a long-suffering look. "Rubbish," he said, and he dropped it into the trash can. "What do you want, Pendleton? A raise? A new title? More responsibility?"

He really didn't listen. Suddenly she felt so tired.

"I don't want any of those things. I want…" She hesitated. She'd never really told him this before, though she'd hinted at it often enough lately. But what good were hints to a man who never listened? Taking a deep breath, she launched into her new anthem of need.

"I want a home. I want a husband. I want babies, and a cat, and long mornings in bed and walks on the beach and..."

He laughed. Far from being offended, she stared at him in wonder. He didn't often laugh right out loud, and when he did, the effect on her pulse rate was astounding. His brilliant white teeth gleamed against his tanned skin, his blue eyes sparkled against the thick, dark lashes, and his face softened for a moment. Laughing made him look so human, so approachable...so sexy. Her heart skipped a beat and a familiar longing rose in her chest, a longing she'd been beating back lately. But it just wouldn't seem to die.

"Pendleton..." Reaching out, he took her chin in his hand and smiled into her eyes.

She smiled back, yearning for him, savoring his touch. That didn't happen very often. He seemed to avoid it most of the time. But maybe he was waking up. Maybe he'd finally seen something in her to care for.

And his gaze did darken as he sobered. He looked more deeply into her eyes and for a moment, he seemed almost puzzled by what he saw there.

"Don't you know that I can't do without you?" he said softly.

Her heart was thumping in her chest. Had he finally noticed?

"You're my other half," he went on. "Without

you I'm pretty good at this business. But together, we knock 'em dead.''

She sighed, shoulders sagging. Business again. She should have known. It was always business with Carter.

"You and I were made for this line of work,'' he told her, dropping his hand from her chin but maintaining his hold on her gaze. "You know I'm right. You're a born negotiator. I've seen your eyes light up when you see a chink in the opposition's armor. I know how cool and silky you get when you know you've found a negotiating ploy that's going to leave the other side gasping. I've seen your elation when we get a settlement that favors TriTerraCorp." He grinned at her, very sure of himself.

He was right. They were very important to their company. TriTerraCorp was a large real-estate development firm with ongoing projects all over the world. The four-story, steel-and-tinted-glass headquarters here in the California central coast town of Rio de Oro was an imposing structure as was fitting for such a consequential corporation.

"And we always get a settlement that favors TriTerraCorp,'' Carter was reminding her. "Because we're the best.''

They *were* the best. He was right. She was good and he was better. He was so good, in fact, that he knew there was a good chance he could manipulate her. She knew it, too.

But she wasn't going to give in that easily this time.

"I'm thirty-two years old, Carter," she told him earnestly. "I'm edging into the zone of no return. If I don't get started on finding someone to have a family with, I won't ever have one."

"Why do you have to quit your job in order to start a family?" he asked her, quite sensibly. "Lots of women keep working."

"Your average job may allow for such things," she said, shaking her head. "Being your sidekick is a little too nonstop for that. I barely have time to breathe. I don't think I could fit in finding a mate and popping out a couple of babies while marking up contracts at the same time with my free hand."

"Babies." He shuddered. "Believe me, you don't want to get mixed up with any of those. Messy, smelly, noisy things. A few all-nighters with a baby will sap all the fight right out of you."

She turned her palms up. "That's exactly what I'm telling you. I can't do both."

Rising from the desk, Carter began to pace restlessly, his hands shoved deep into his pockets. She was being more tenacious than usual. She might actually mean it this time. He couldn't let that happen. He couldn't lose her. Somehow over the past two years, their work patterns had become so intertwined, he couldn't imagine setting up a series of important negotiations without her.

He looked at her sideways. Why hadn't he seen this coming? He made it a practice to keep his distance, even from Pendleton. He'd learned early in life that human relationships always ended badly. It didn't pay to let your heart get involved, not if you wanted to avoid getting it broken. Life was so much safer when you cruised the surface instead of plunging down into the deep.

He'd made a promise to himself never to let anyone become so important that his happiness depended upon keeping them in his life. Bad things happened when you did that. And yet, here he was, on the verge of losing her, and scared it just might happen.

Oh, what the hell! He could go on without her. He could get another associate, train her just the way he'd trained Pendleton. It would work out fine. No one was indispensable.

And then he turned and looked at her, took in her porcelain-fine profile, her beautiful blond hair, her trim figure, the graceful curve of her neck, and something seemed to quiver deep inside him. He couldn't lose her.

"Not so fast, Pendleton," he said calmly. "I don't think you've thought this through. There are things in the works that could change your mind."

She shook her head. "There will always be something coming up that would tempt me to stay," she admitted. "I love working here and you know it.

But my full nature isn't fulfilled with work. I need more.''

He nodded dismissively and his face took on a pensive look.

"I talked to the Joliet Aire people this morning," he told her with exaggerated casualness. "And Monsieur Jobert has agreed to meet with you."

Her head snapped up and she stared at him. "What?" Monsieur Jobert was an illusive contact she'd been going after for six months. She jumped up, facing Carter and beaming. "You're kidding!"

He nodded, gratified by her delighted surprise. "It's true. That is exactly what we're going to Paris for. He finally read one of your letters and wants to meet the lady behind the persuasive words."

"I knew I could get to him eventually," she said, eyes shining with triumph, her hand tightened in a little fist. "Now, to make sure I've got the right ammunition to convince him once we meet face-to-face..." Her voice trailed off as she realized what she was saying.

He studied her closely, one eyebrow cocked. "One more trip to Paris, Pendleton," he said softly. "Come on. You know you can't pass this one up."

She turned away, thinking hard. He'd won again. But still, an interview with the famous Monsieur Jobert!

Carter watched her, his eyes filled with worry now that she wasn't gazing into his. The last thing in the world he could afford was to lose Amy Pen-

dleton. Together they were a well-oiled machine.
Their successes were legendary at TriTerraCorp.

Besides, there was a part of him, deep down, a
tiny part he didn't often allow to surface, that would
miss her in other ways. No, he couldn't do without
her. His throat tightened as he thought of it. He'd
already lost too much, dammit. This was someone
he wasn't going to let walk out of his life.

"All right," she said, turning back to look at him
with stormy eyes. "One more trip to Paris. But after
that…"

"*Après moi le déluge,*" he said, grinning at her
as he repeated the famous quote attributed to Louis
XV. "'After me the deluge!'"

She laughed softly, shaking her head, not sure
what the quote had to do with anything, but enjoying
it anyway—enjoying him.

And that was part of her problem. She just enjoyed him too darn much! And that spoiled the rest
of the male population for her. Every man she met
she compared to Carter, and every other man came
up wanting when she made those comparisons.

"More like, 'after Paris, the resignation'," she
corrected him, her eyes sparkling. "Don't forget.
I'm quitting."

He didn't answer but his confident smile told her
he would be working on new ways to keep her from
doing that. And he was very good at orchestrating
outcomes the way he liked them.

* * *

" 'The more you try to get out, the more they pull you back in'," Meg quoted in her best mobster accent.

Amy laughed at her sister's impression of a gangster. She'd always been a natural actress, even when they were both growing up together in San Diego. Amy remembered the neighborhood productions they had put on, with Meg playing most of the parts and other children drafted off the street to play against her. Amy herself was usually the set designer, promoter, ticket-taker and prompter. While Meg loved being in front of an audience, Amy had always preferred the behind-the-scenes activities.

"That's about the size of it," she admitted. "But I'm going to quit right after we get back from this trip. Honest."

"Good." Meg smiled at her sister. Only two years older, she'd considered herself the head of the family, ever since their parents had died a few years before. "Because, you've got to admit," she went on, "you're not getting any younger, Amy."

Meg filled a little bowl with homemade strawberry ice cream and placed it on the kitchen table in front of her sister, then went on to fill two more tiny bowls.

Amy bit her tongue, taking up the ice cream and grabbing a spoon to eat it with, but fuming inside. What a dumb thing that was to say. Of course she wasn't getting any younger. Nobody was. Meg might as well advise her to breathe air.

Still, she held back her temper and didn't let her sister see how much she resented that comment. After all, she knew Meg was just trying to help her. She was concerned, and she wanted Amy to find a man and have the happiness she'd found with her husband Tim and her three little children.

Amy loved her sister. Looking at her now, with her common-sense attitude and her shiny auburn hair cut in a short bob, she felt a surge of affection. She really felt as though she'd neglected Meg over the past few years. She was on the road so much, she barely had time to stop by for holidays like Christmas and Thanksgiving before racing off again to go to cities all over the world. Sometimes she felt that she hardly knew Meg's little ones, and she regretted that.

"Besides, if you quit, you'll have more time to date." Meg turned and gave her a bright smile that failed in its attempt to seem offhandedly casual. "Paul is always asking about you."

Paul was Meg's neighbor, a perfectly nice man Amy had met over dinner at her sister's. But she had to hold back her reaction once again, because while Paul was pleasant and had a certain charm, he was no Carter James.

Still, whom was she kidding? Carter was exactly the man she couldn't get. Maybe Paul was more her speed. That is, if she really wanted to settle down and have a family.

"Deedee!" Meg called as she set out the two little bowls. "Scamp! Ice cream!"

A sound very much like that of stampeding cattle came thundering through the house and two very small children exploded into the room. The boy was a towhead with hair like flax. The little girl had a mop of chocolate-colored curls. They stopped dead when they caught sight of Amy. Deedee, all of eighteen months or so, reached out and clung to her four-year-old brother's arm while they both stared, wide-eyed.

"It's your aunt Amy, sillies," Meg exclaimed with a short laugh. "Come give her a kiss."

There was just no way that was going to happen. Amy could see it in their eyes.

"Hi, Deedee," she said cheerfully, though she heard the oddly uncomfortable note in her own voice. And if she heard it, she knew darn well they did. "How are you, Scamp?"

"Fine."

Scamp, whose real name was William, answered her but didn't look eager to make physical contact. He put his arm around his little sister's shoulders as though to protect her, and they both sidled away from their aunt, trying to reach the table without having to come within arm's reach of their unfamiliar relative. And they got away with it, since Meg didn't notice. She had turned away and was chattering on about something she'd seen in the paper that morning.

Amy felt her smile harden like concrete around her mouth. The children hated her. And she had no idea how to charm them. Why wouldn't they be wary? They grabbed their dishes of ice cream and made tracks out of the room, glancing back with half smiles, then ducking their heads and disappearing. Here she was dressed to the hilt, on her way to the airport to leave for Paris. They'd never seen her like this before, in heels and a power suit, with the obligatory silk power scarf, and her hair combed back severely into a twist held by a diamond-studded comb. She even had on her power makeup, which could almost be considered a mask. All necessary for striking tremulous awe in the hearts of negotiating adversaries, but hardly the thing to endear nieces and nephews.

There was that, and the fact that she hadn't been around enough lately for them to be holding many fond memories. Why did she let herself get so caught up in business that she neglected her family? She wasn't going to let that happen any longer. She was going to pick a time and come over every week. Right after she got back from Paris.

She groaned softly, realizing how that sounded like putting things off again. She'd done too much of that. Could she change?

She finished off the ice cream and sighed as she pushed the dish away. Well, there you had it. She was frightening to small children. Was this the future she wanted? It was down to the wire and it was her choice. She *had* to change.

"I'd better get going if I don't want to miss the flight," she said, rising and giving her pretty sister a kiss on the cheek.

"Remember," Meg said stoutly, gripping her by the shoulders and gazing intently into her eyes. "You're committed. You're going to quit when you get back from Paris."

Amy nodded, frowning with mock ferocity, and they both laughed as she went out the door, waving. But the laugh faded quickly as she made her way to her car.

Life without Carter. Was it possible?

But she did want to have a normal life and a family, and if she was serious about that, it was time to attack her problem with the right sort of focus and attention.

Suppose she took some time off and tried to get this done. What would it take? At least six months to find someone suitable and congenial whom she might want to marry. Another six months to really get to know him—and convince him that he wanted to marry, as well. Another six months to set up the wedding. Then a few months before getting pregnant...

She gasped in horror as she turned into the airport parking lot. It would take almost three years, from the moment she began her project, to the point where she could possibly have a baby in her arms.

She was going to be a hundred years old before she got there!

It all seemed so hopeless. And as she stood waiting for the shuttle to take her to the international terminal, it did occur to her that there might be an indication of the root of her problem in the fact that she even thought about things like this in a business-like manner—projecting time frames and plotting out an attack the way she would plot out a business move. She'd been too long in the business world, hadn't she?

She saw Carter waiting for her by the ticket counter and her heart leaped up as it always did when she saw him. She loved the way he stood, so casually sure of himself, so sure the world was his oyster. If only he were the marrying kind. If only he would somehow magically, suddenly, fall in love with her. That would take care of everything.

She sighed, then started forward, walking quickly to join him.

"Darn you, Carter," she was saying under her breath. "Why don't you love me?"

Chapter Two

One week later

Carter shifted his weight restlessly as he stood waiting for Amy outside the ICU unit of the Monte Vista Hospital. He hated the look of the place—the anonymous white walls, the stainless-steel appliances. He hated the mysterious sounds, the jarring smells. Even the pretty redhead giving him the eye from behind the nurses' station didn't make things any better. Every instinct he owned was screaming at him to run for it. As far as he was concerned, only bad things happened in hospitals. He'd had these feelings ever since, as a boy, he'd watched his mother die in one.

Ordinarily, he shunned them like the plague. But this visit had been unavoidable. The moment he'd

heard the announcement paging Amy as they
stepped into the terminal at the airport, disembarking
the flight from Paris, a knot had pulled up hard in
his stomach and it hadn't yet let go.

They had raced to a phone and the message had
been bad. Just hours before, Amy's sister and her
husband had been in a terrible car accident. They'd
been hit by a drunk driver. Both were in critical
condition. Carter would never forget the look on
Amy's face as she absorbed the news.

They had raced to the hospital and found that both
injured parties were in surgery. Amy had turned to
him, her face stricken and questioning—as though
he could stop all this from happening somehow—
and he'd wanted to do something big and grand to
make it all go away for her, to protect her. But there
was nothing he could do but stay with her, and that's
what he did.

Not that she seemed to notice most of the time.
For the most part, she had sat huddled in a chair in
the lobby, staring at the far wall. She'd looked up
when he'd brought her a cup of water, looked up
and smiled absently at him and thanked him. And
then went back to staring at the wall. He watched
her, feeling helpless and frustrated.

He could see her now through the glass partition-
ing off the ICU unit, bending over her sister as she
lay in the bed, leaning close to kiss her gently, then
turning toward the exit. Carter straightened. Maybe
he could finally get her out of here.

She came out through the swinging doors and he winced as his gaze swept over her. Her eyes were huge and clouded with anguish. The dark smudges beneath them, the tension in her face, all told him things didn't look particularly rosy right now.

"What do they say?" he asked, falling in beside her as she walked the corridor toward the elevator. "What's the prognosis?"

She glanced at him as though surprised to find him there. "Oh. Carter." She stopped and looked up at him. "Carter, what are you still doing here?"

"I wanted to..." He hesitated and shrugged, his eyes hooded. "To take care of you."

"To take care of me." A bittersweet smile played at her lips. "Oh, Carter, you should know me well enough by now. I can take care of myself."

"Hmm." His mouth twisted, but he wasn't going to remind her of the basket case she'd been just a few hours before.

"Well, at least they are sure Meg and Tim will pull through. Their conditions have both stabilized. But they will have to be hospitalized for..." She swallowed hard and forced herself to continue. "For weeks, maybe months. Tim's back was broken. And Meg—" Her face crumpled suddenly. "Both legs broken..." she managed to whisper, shaking her head, her fist to her mouth.

Carter stared at her, feeling helpless and angry with himself. He wanted to take her in his arms. He wanted to comfort her, to tell her everything was

going to be all right. It shouldn't be this hard. All
he had to do was reach out...

He raised a hand awkwardly, ready to pat her
shoulder. But she moved away without noticing and
he let his hand drop. Something cold and painful
filled his chest.

"No," she was telling herself fiercely, closing her
eyes and fighting back the tears. "I will not cry. I
can't cry." Straightening her shoulders, she frowned
at him. "I'm the one who has to take care of things.
I will not cry," she promised.

Carter shrugged, shoving his hands deep into his
pockets and trying to look casual. "Go ahead and
cry," he said gruffly. "I'd say it's a crying situation."

"But I don't have time for that," she was saying
briskly, wiping her eyes and heading for the elevator. "I've got to go to the children."

He blinked, trailing behind her. "The children?"

She nodded, jabbing at the down button. "Meg's
children. Deedee and Scamp and Jillian, the baby."

"Oh."

He relaxed. Meg's children. Of course. Arrangements would have to be made. He could help her
with that. He knew people who would know of a
good child-care agency. A few phone calls should
do the trick. His spirits brightened and he looked
forward to doing this for her. It would make him
feel a little more useful.

The elevator arrived and they boarded side by side.

"Those poor babies," Amy was saying. "They must be so scared. Thank God they weren't in the car when the accident occurred."

He looked at her, barely hearing her words. He'd always liked the way she looked and for some reason, she was especially fetching right now with her lipstick rubbed off and her eyes so huge. Another impulse to offer her something more in the way of physical comfort rose in him, but he fought it back. They'd made it through two years and he'd managed to keep from letting their relationship get personal. This was no time to let his defenses weaken.

Pendleton was the best associate he'd ever worked with, more a partner than an employee. Together they made magic in the business world. If he allowed his natural inclinations to lead him to a romance with her, all that would be ruined. Once emotional elements were allowed to enter into it, the balance would be destroyed and disaster would be lurking just around the corner.

No touching.

That was his golden rule. He'd had enough experience to know that romance never lasted and, when it was over, what had once been sweet quickly turned to bitter ashes.

They'd gone through a rough patch for a while. She'd definitely been attracted to him and she'd let him know it. He'd thought at first there would be no real problem, as she wasn't really his type. But then he'd realized she wasn't really any type at all. She was just darn good at business, and darn appealing to his male spirit. He'd needed the strength of Hercules to resist her, and there had been times he'd almost succumbed.

What doesn't kill you makes you stronger.

That was another of his watch phrases. He'd come up through some hard times in his youth and he'd repeated that phrase whenever his situation seemed almost too much to bear. Now he told himself those words whenever the temptation to take Pendleton in his arms was almost overwhelming. He wasn't sure if it really applied, but it always made him feel better.

Right now she was lifting her face to him and his breath stopped in his throat. The need to kiss those beautiful lips crashed though him like a summer storm. He stared down at her, only minimally aware that she was speaking.

"Meg was conscious for a while and I got to talk to her," she said.

Carter blinked, catching hold of himself and looking quickly away so that he could breathe again.

"That sounds like a good sign," he muttered, hoping she hadn't noticed his minor lapse.

"Yes, I think so." She sighed and he realized she looked close to the end of her rope.

"Why don't we go eat?" he suggested. It had

been hours since their last meal, and that had been airplane food.

"Eat?" She wrinkled her nose. "I don't think I can eat."

He gave her a halfhearted grin. "Well, you could watch me."

She patted his arm. "No thanks. I'm going to have to get out to Meg's house," she said, turning away.

"Meg's house?"

"The children," she reminded him just a bit impatiently.

They left the elevator together and both turned automatically toward the parking lot.

"I promised Meg I would go out and take care of them right away." She shook her head. "That was the only thing she could think about and she could hardly force out the words, but I knew what she meant. All she cares about is those kids."

She sighed. "Poor little things. And now they are going to be saddled with an aunt they barely know instead of their mother and father." She remembered how they had reacted to her just days before and bit her lip. How was she going to win them over?

"Where do they live?"

"Just outside of town, in the Las Palmas Valley. It's probably ten minutes from here."

Carter frowned. "Listen, you don't have to do that. I can make a few calls, get someone to handle this. I know some very good sources. We can get expert care out there immediately.''

Amy stopped dead and turned to look up at him, realization dawning in her gaze. "Carter, I don't think you understand. I'm the one who is going to 'handle' this. I'm going to take care of them for the duration. I'm the only one available to do it.''

His brows came together. Something told him he wasn't going to like the plans she was making.

"That's absurd. You're not a baby-sitter.'' His glance was scathing. "You're a businesswoman. You don't do diapers. And believe me, you don't want to.''

"Oh, Carter. How do you know?''

"You'd be surprised,'' he muttered, scanning the lot and spotting their cars, parked together in the next area.

He nodded in the direction they needed to go and began to lead her there. "Where are the children now?'' he asked.

"I think a neighbor has them. I have to check on that.''

"Then let the neighbor take care of them,'' he began, but she stopped short again and faced him.

"No, Carter. I will not let the neighbor take care of them. They are my family and my responsibility.''

"But we have the Northridge situation to look into in the morning,'' he said, looking as though he just didn't get why she would prefer the company of children to the fast-paced atmosphere they both thrived in. "You know that's going to blow up on us if we don't take care of the details right away."

"You're going to have to take care of it on your own," she told him firmly. Then she hesitated, knowing it was time to make him face what she knew he didn't want to. "Carter..." She put her hand on his arm and searched his eyes, wishing she could think of a way to soften the blow. "Carter, come to grips with this," she said softly. "I won't be in tomorrow. I won't be in the day after."

He laughed shortly. "But you will be in the day after that. Two good days of child-care duty and you'll be begging for an emergency assignment."

"No. I won't." She pushed her hair back behind her ear and looked at him sideways. "This has been coming for a long time. You know that. I've made it clear, I think. And now any decision has really been taken out of my hands. I have no choice. And neither do you." She smiled tremulously. "You do realize what this means, don't you?"

"No," he said stubbornly, avoiding her gaze, looking restlessly into the parking lot. "What?"

"I'm not going to be working for you anymore, Carter. I warned you."

His head swung around and he stared at her, stunned. She was making it sound as though it was final. He'd been prepared for a short break in her presence at work, but nothing permanent.

Oh, sure, she'd been threatening to quit, and even

written up resignations to taunt him with, but he'd never taken her seriously. He had always been sure that she valued their collaboration as much as he did. Now he was beginning to realize she was talking about a complete abandonment of her responsibilities. That just couldn't be. What was he going to do without her?

"What are you talking about?" he asked, his voice low, his gaze intense.

She took a shaky breath. "I promised my sister I would take care of her children."

He nodded tersely. "Of course you did. And we'll spare no expense in finding the best child care—"

"No." She shook her head adamantly. "I'm not going to leave them with strangers. I'm going to move into Meg's house and be with those children night and day until their mother and father are well enough to come home to them."

"We'll see how long you last," he said, managing to look more confident than he felt.

Shaking her head, she gave an exasperated sigh and said, "Carter, read my lips. I quit!"

Their gazes held for a long moment. Then she turned on her heel and left him.

Carter watched her walk toward where the car was parked, and for a moment, he couldn't move.

This was not possible. There had to be another way. Why he couldn't think of something right now, he wasn't sure. Maybe he was too jet-lagged. Maybe he was just too unprepared for such a thing as was happening. In any case, his mind was fuzzy and his stomach was growling and he didn't have a clue how he was going to get her back in the office. He only knew he was going to do it. Because he had to.

Amy lay very still, staring at what she could see of the ceiling. There it was again. A scratching sound. She knew what it was, what it had to be. But that didn't make it any less chilling to hear.

Scratch, scratch. Scuffle, scuffle. Fred was riffling through the closed closet. And she knew it was going to be her job to catch him.

The children had told her about Fred the day before.

"He's gone!" Scamp had cried, his eyes huge and filled with horror. "I on'y left the door open fer a little to get him water and he go'd away!" He'd clutched her around the knees, tears threatening. "Aun' Amy, don' let that mean ole cat get him!"

Fred was a white mouse. A very pretty little mouse, from what she'd heard. But Fred was on the lam.

Amy shuddered. She didn't have a lot of experience at catching little white mice. A nice trap would have been her preference. But this was a beloved pet, so traps were out. She was going to have to catch him carefully, so as not to hurt him. How the heck was she supposed to do that?

Sighing, she rolled onto her side and closed her

eyes, firmly determined to get a little more sleep before another day broke over her like a giant ocean wave. That was what the day before had felt like—surfing on the big ones at Makaha Beach—something way beyond her experience and capabilities.

Taking care of children wasn't as simple as it seemed. Oh, she'd known it wouldn't be all that easy. But she hadn't realized caring for them would leave her drained, both physically and emotionally, and wondering how most mothers did it.

But women *did* do it, and most did it very well. In bygone ages, they did it without modern plumbing and washing machines and fast-food restaurants. Could you imagine? Not even *Sesame Street*. What she had was a cakewalk compared to what most women had gone through over the ages.

But that only made her feel even worse. If she was having this much trouble when it was so much easier than it had ever been in history, what did that say about her?

Oh, grow up, she told herself impatiently, rejecting the impulse toward self-pity. After all, she'd only been doing this for a little more than twenty-four hours now.

She'd raced over and collected the children from where they were being kept that first night. Paul Hanford, the man Meg had been trying to get her interested in, was the neighbor taking care of them. She'd taken the steps up onto his front porch slowly, feeling a lot of trepidation, anxious that the children wouldn't want to go with her, and that she would have a hard time getting them to accept her as their interim parent. After all, the last time they'd seen her they hadn't actually been brimming with friendliness toward her.

But when the chips were down, they had surprised her.

"Aun' Amy!" Scamp had cried, peering though his wispy bangs of white-blond hair when she'd appeared in the doorway of Paul's house. "Deedee, it's Aun' Amy!"

And the two children had run to her, with Scamp actually throwing his arms around her knees with so much force he'd just about knocked her down.

"I guess blood really is thicker than water," she'd murmured to herself as she went down on one knee to embrace them both.

A warm feeling of affection curled through her, along with a strong sense of empathy for two young ones who had to be scared and very confused about what had happened to their parents. She must look like a comfortingly familiar face under these circumstances. And luckily, she wasn't dressed to kill—in a business sense—as she had been days before. They'd at least recognized her for who she was.

"Hey, I just talked to your mother," she told them, brushing Scamp's hair back off his forehead and noticing, suddenly, how much like her sister he looked.

Pictures in albums saved from the childhood she

and Meg had shared portrayed a little girl whose face was a very close model for this young boy in front of her. That made her want to hug him again.

"Your mother sends you her love and she promises to be home just as soon as she can."

"Does she have a boo-boo?" Scamp asked solemnly.

Amy nodded, blinking quickly to hold back the tears that threatened to come again. "She has a bunch of boo-boos. And so does your daddy. The doctor is going to fix them right up, though. So don't you worry."

Scamp thought about that for a moment. "I got a boo-boo on my arm," he offered at last, showing her the scab. "Is that like Daddy's?"

Amy hesitated, then smiled at him. "Sort of," she allowed. "Just a little worse."

Scamp nodded wisely, showing he understood. "Are you gonna take care of us, Aun' Amy?" he asked her, his blue eyes hopeful.

"Of course," she told them, smiling warmly. "I'll stay with you until your mother comes home. I promise."

Deedee sighed happily and cuddled in close, while Scamp pulled back, seeming to suddenly remember that he had his young male pride to consider.

"I'm really glad you're going to be able to do this," Paul told her, smiling down at the picture she made with the little dark-haired girl in her arms.

"I've got a sales trip to Omaha tomorrow and I won't be back for three or four days. Otherwise, I would have been glad to take over for Tim and Meg."

"Oh, no," Amy said quickly. "They're my family. I'll take care of them." She hugged Deedee closer, then put her on her little feet. "Run get your things, kids. I'm going to take you home."

She rose, waiting for the children to leave the room before saying quietly to Paul, "I really haven't heard all the details yet. Where were they when the accident happened? And where were Meg and Tim going? Do you know?"

Paul nodded. He was a pleasant-looking man with slightly thinning blond hair and a nice smile. "They were going to lunch to celebrate Tim's promotion. Did you know his law firm just made him a partner?"

"No," she said softly, feeling again a sense of having been woefully inattentive to what was going on in her sister's life. "How great for him." She swallowed. "So the kids were at home?"

"Yes. Cheryl Park, an older lady from down the street, was sitting with them. But she had to get home, so I took over and brought them over here."

"Thank you so much," she said earnestly, holding out a hand to shake his. "I—we all appreciate it. You've been a big help."

"Any time," he said, holding her hand a little too long and beaming at her significantly. "As soon as

I get back from Omaha, I'll be able to help a lot more."

Her smile wavered as she witnessed the intensity of his and she pulled her hand away.

"Yes," she said quickly. "Well..." She turned, looking toward where the baby slept in a travel chair. "I guess I'd better get them home. It must be way past their bedtime by now."

"Yes, of course." He looked pleased with something and she wasn't sure why.

Deedee and Scamp came running up, ready to go home. Amy helped Deedee into her sweater.

"'Bye, Pooky," Scamp called back at the huge orange-colored cat sitting on a pillow in the far corner of the room. "See ya tomorrow."

"'Bye, 'bye," Deedee said, copying her brother and waving at the animal.

The cat blinked its golden eyes and lashed its tiger-striped tail and didn't say a thing.

"I'll come with you," Paul offered. "I'll help you carry the baby, help you get the other two to bed." He gave Amy a comforting smile. "You'll need help, all right. They are a handful."

"Are they?" Suddenly her confidence began to show some wear around the edges. Was she going to be up to this job? She'd never taken care of children before, never even baby-sat as a teenager. She was always too busy entering competitions and running for class office to have time for things like that.

And she hadn't visited with Meg and her crew

often enough to get a feel for it. Whenever she was over, Meg was a whirlwind of activity, usually ordering Amy just to sit and talk to her, tell her everything about what it was like to live in the fast-paced business world.

"Oh, sure," Paul said happily as he headed out on the porch, baby in tow. "They're not bad kids, mind you, but they are very, very active. But don't worry. You'll get the hang of it right away."

"Will I?" she had whispered to herself as she followed with the older children. "And what happens if I don't?"

Snapping out of her reverie, Amy willed herself to drift off to sleep. She knew she'd need all her energy to face another day.

Chapter Three

You'll get the hang of it, Amy told herself encouragingly as she watched the morning sun begin to form a light pattern on the bedroom wall. *Just give it some time.*

But there was no more time—the baby was stirring. She could hear the little murmurs that would soon grow into a full-throated cry. For just a moment she longed for her usual mornings, awakening to her clock radio, lingering over coffee and the newspaper, dressing in something sharp and business-like and arriving at the office in time to get a morning glance, along with a cynical comment or two, from a suave and debonair Carter.

Carter. She felt an ache of regret that twisted inside her. Instead of that grown-up, sophisticated way to start her day, she had to share a bedroom with a noisy white mouse. There had been a time when she'd dreamed of sharing such a room with Carter.

But the baby's noises were getting more insistent. No time for nostalgia. Sighing, she threw back the covers and rolled out of bed. Time to start the day.

"Carter, we really have to get the final numbers on the Milan estimate. They've been calling all week and I put them off because you were in France, but they know you're back and..."

Carter looked up from the papers he'd been staring at and frowned at Delia, his secretary. Middle-aged and motherly, she ran the office with a fine efficiency and attention to detail; she liked her boss a lot, but didn't necessarily approve of everything he did.

"I don't have those numbers," he told her. "Pendleton was working on those."

"I've looked through her desk, but I can't find them." Delia waited expectantly, her large brown eyes earnest.

He hesitated, then shrugged impatiently. "Give her a call," he suggested.

Delia set her lips and put her hands on her hips. "Mr. James, I will not bother her with office business. She doesn't work here anymore. We have to do this without her."

Carter stared out across the room at the desk where his administrative associate was supposed to be. There was an interloper sitting in her chair. A short, eager young woman with a head of bouncing red curls sat looking through files where Pendleton ought to be. He had an impulse to growl like a guard dog seeing an intruder, but he reined it in and managed to speak calmly to his secretary.

"I'll work on the Milan figures later," he told Delia. He held up a piece of onionskin-thin paper. "Right now I need someone to interpret what this letter from the Lee Group in Singapore is all about."

"Well, give it to Martha. If she's going to be your associate, she's going to have to learn to do these things."

He gazed at Delia as though she'd advised him to call in a palm reader.

"She won't have a clue," he told her scornfully. "Pendleton was the only one who ever knew what these screwballs were saying."

Delia shrugged. "She'll have to learn sometime. And you're going to have to teach her."

He groaned, almost writhing in his chair.

"You taught Amy," Delia reminded him sternly. "She didn't know anything at first, either."

"Maybe not," he rumbled. "But she had an instinct for the business like no one I'd ever seen before. I'll never find anyone else like her."

Delia threw up her hands. "You *are* resistant to change, aren't you?"

Change? Was that what he was resistant to? He scowled at the woman. What was she so cheery about, anyway? She was going to miss Pendleton, too. He couldn't believe she thought this Martha person was a fitting replacement any more than he did.

"Oh, she'll do fine, in time," Delia assured him as though she'd read his mind. She turned to leave. "Give her a chance," she flung back over her shoulder.

He didn't want to give her a chance. He wanted Pendleton back. He wanted to look out across the room and see her sleek blond head bent over a problem, see her jump up in excitement when she'd figured out an answer, see her striding toward his desk with a look of triumph on her beautiful lips... Where the hell was she, anyway?

Looking out at where she ought to be, he felt something painful in his chest. "Gas pain," he told himself hopefully. "I'll get over it." But he knew better.

The day seemed to drag. Even sparring with his nemesis in Finance, Gary Brown, tight-fisted holder of the travel advance purse strings, didn't perk him up much. He spent an inordinate amount of time staring at the telephone and thinking of different things he needed to say to Pendleton. But he couldn't call her. That would be like...well, like admitting defeat or something.

Or admitting that you need her, said a little voice in his head.

But he'd already admitted that. In fact, he'd pretty

much taken out billboards to make sure she got the message. So why not call her? Why not?

And then Martha, his new associate, was coming toward his desk, a look of eager expectation on her cute little face. She was so young, so earnest, so...so un-Pendleton.

"Mr. James," she said brightly, her smile fixed. "I need to find a file on land prices in Australia. It's listed in the file index but it's not where it's supposed to be."

Ignoring the smile, he frowned at her. "We were just using that file recently. Have you checked the copy room? Someone might have left it in the copy machine."

"That was the very first place I looked."

His frown began to fade. "Have you looked through the desk?"

"Yes, sir. Twice."

Carter leaned back in his chair. He glanced out at where Delia usually sat. Her desk was empty. A faint smile began to play at the corners of his wide mouth.

"I guess we'll have to call Pendleton," he said slowly. "I can't see what else we can do." He gave his new associate the first genuine smile she'd ever seen from him. "But there's no need for you to bother about it. You just go on back and do some typing or something." He sat up straight in his chair and flexed his shoulders. "I'll make the call."

Martha blinked at him uncertainly, then quickly

went back to her desk. Carter stared at the telephone for a long moment, anticipating, then reached for it.

Amy felt like a woman under siege. If yesterday had been difficult, today was impossible. It had started out badly and just gotten worse.

The only high point had been a call to the hospital that told her Meg and Tim were improving steadily and might be able to take phone calls in another day or two. What a relief it was to know they were probably going to be all right.

But from there on it was all downhill.

The baby woke up fussing and had kept it up all day. She wouldn't eat, wouldn't sleep, only wanted to be held and carried around. Amy's arms still ached from that activity. She'd finally had to put Jillian down, letting her fuss all to herself. But the sound of her wails was like the constant scraping of fingernails across a blackboard and she wasn't sure how much more she could take. Luckily, the baby's crying subsided after a while.

Scamp had decided at breakfast that the only way he wanted to communicate was by barking like a dog from now on. One bark meant yes, two meant no. The trouble was, he loved the barking so much, he usually went on and on until it was darn hard to figure out what he was trying to say. Amy had pretty much given up trying.

She'd tried to lose her cares in laundry work, but someone had left a crayon in a shirt pocket and the entire washload ended up stained with purple streaks by the time she'd pulled it out of the dryer.

"Oh, no," she moaned, looking at the ruined clothing. There would be no way to hide this. Humiliation was dogging her now.

The kids had turned up their noses at the sandwiches she'd made for lunch. It was disconcerting to get bad reviews from children who barely knew the English language.

Shortly thereafter, Deedee found her mother's perfume and used it generously. Now the bathroom reeked of Bewitched and might never lose that scent again. Amy had scolded her, then given her a quick bath, which was only moderately successful in restoring her little-girl smell. Then she'd sent her to her room, where she could now be found holding on to her blanket and sobbing, "Mommy...Mommy... Mommy" over and over as she rocked herself in her time-out misery.

During all this, Scamp had been barking at her until she thought she would go mad, but when she had a sudden lapse in patience and spoke shortly to him, his crestfallen look made her bite her tongue and scold herself until she felt as bad as he looked.

She decided to bake cookies to cheer them all up. She knew how to bake cookies. She'd done that before, even though it had been years.

But she must have lost the knack somehow, because what she ended up with was very much like an industrial form of glue, burned on the bottom and raw on top and the children wouldn't touch them. Not that she blamed them. Neither would she.

She'd been avoiding the issue all day, but it finally came out and hit her right between the eyes. The evidence was beginning to pile up. She was a complete failure at this child-care business.

When the telephone rang, she glared at it as though it were just another disaster waiting to pounce. And truth to tell, she didn't feel as though she could handle much more.

"Hello?" she said, bracing for the worst.

"Rebecca of Sunnybrook Farm, please."

"Carter!"

Carter's voice was like a siren song from a previous and beloved chapter of her existence. He sounded so good! Her eyes welled with tears. "Oh, Carter!"

"Pendleton? What is it? What's wrong?"

His voice vibrated with real concern and she couldn't hold back a little sob.

"Pendleton, what's happened? I'm coming over there. I'll be there in..."

"No." She smiled through her tears, feeling a wave of affection for the man. Good old Carter. "No, really, don't come over. It's...it's just that everything's been going wrong and it's so good to hear a friendly voice." She sniffed and got control of herself. "Hey, this child-rearing stuff is really hard," she wailed. "I had no idea."

"Well, if I were a lesser man, I would probably

be saying 'I told you so' about now," he noted dryly. "But from your tone, I gather that sort of thing wouldn't be taken in the proper spirit, so I'll resist."

She grinned. Even his teasing seemed welcome at this point. "Thank you, Carter," she told him. "I appreciate your sensitivity."

"By all means." He paused, then said firmly, "So, when are you coming back to work?"

She didn't feel quite the outrage she knew she should. A quiet business office seemed like an oasis in a noisy world right now. Still, she had to let him know there was no hope.

"I'm in this for the long haul, Carter. This is where I belong right now, and I'm going to stay."

"No matter how bad it gets?"

"No matter how bad it gets," she repeated back to him, though she had to swallow hard.

"But it's all so unnecessary, Pendleton. There are people who are trained and experienced in child care who could be doing a much better job..."

"But it's *my* job. And I'm going to get better at it. Honestly. I am."

"You have a job you are already the best at..."

A shriek from the family room set her nerves jangling. "Oh...oh," she said into the mouthpiece. "Sorry, Carter. Gotta go."

Slamming down the receiver, she ran into the family room to find Scamp pulling his sister's hair, attempting to take over possession of a plush stuffed penguin that Deedee had her little fingers sunk into tightly. Just another episode in the constantly running adventure that was her life. She pulled the two of them apart and tried to find a toy that would satisfy each of them. It was only later that she thought to wonder about what Carter had called for.

Carter hung up the telephone with a slight smile on his face. He hadn't got the information he needed, but that was all right.

"It will just give me an excuse to call again," he murmured to himself. "I'll give her…oh, say about two hours. Things ought to be going wild about four in the afternoon. Meanwhile I'll see if I can't come up with an argument to win her over to my side of things. There's got to be one." Leaning back in his chair, he put his feet up on the desk and smiled. It was only a matter of time.

But by four o'clock, the time when Carter had figured Amy would be going crazy, things had changed.

A small miracle had happened, and both Deedee and Scamp were down for naps and actually asleep for a change, and the baby was snoozing, as well. Amy sat with a cup of tea and let each muscle relax, one at a time. A heavenly respite…until the telephone rang.

Sighing, she answered it.

"Carter." She wasn't really surprised to hear his

voice and she had to admit, she rather liked it that he was calling. "Again?"

"Yes, I need some information. Think you can get a moment of peace so that you can help me?"

"Why of course," she said calmly. "Everything is fine here. I can give you all the time you need."

He hesitated, obviously astonished by her sudden tranquility, and she smiled. Astonishing Carter wasn't easy. But it was so very, very satisfying.

"Well, I'm glad," he said, though he didn't sound completely convinced. "But listen, we can't find the file with those Australian land prices you researched last month. Any ideas where it might be?"

"Oh, sure." She sat up straight, glad to think office thoughts for a moment. "I put it in with the statistics I was preparing for the Northridge people. Someone needs to put together a report incorporating all that information into a readable form and..."

She paused. What was she doing? It was no longer her job. "Anyway, that's where it is."

On the other end of the line, Carter tilted his chair back and narrowed his eyes. "Okay, thanks," he said slowly, feeling his way. "Has everything settled down there? You don't seem to be your old hysterical self."

She rolled her eyes and made a face at the receiver. "Everything is under control," she told him smoothly. "Every job has a learning curve, you know. I think I'm getting a handle on this one."

"Hmm." He sounded skeptical. "Well, things are not quite so hunky-dory here. We're really having a lot of trouble tying up your loose ends." He paused to let that sink in, then went on. "After all, you didn't have the usual two-week period of winding down and getting your work in the proper shape for someone new to take over, much less train anyone to do things the way you would have them done."

"Oh, Carter," she said, feeling guilty—knowing that was exactly what he was trying to make her do, but feeling that way nonetheless. "I know. I was thinking about that last night. I do owe you. I'm really sorry, but it can't be helped at this point."

He let a moment of silence speak volumes, then continued to set his trap. "I was thinking. The situation is a real mess. And I know you are very busy rocking babies and all—vital work, I'm not knocking it—but there must be some way you can help."

She sighed. She knew he was leading up to something and she knew it was going to be something that would be hard for her to comply with. Otherwise he wouldn't be taking this roundabout way of expressing himself. It amused her that she knew him so well that she could see these things coming.

"If you can think of something, I'd be glad to do it. I really do feel an obligation to make the transition as smooth as possible." She shrugged, thinking but not coming up with anything much. "But, Carter, I just don't see what I can do."

"I've had a thought."

She laughed softly. *Oh, I'll just bet you have,* she thought to herself. "Really?" she said aloud. "What is that?"

"You could get a sitter for the kids and come in half a day."

She thought about it for a moment. It really wasn't such an outrageous request. "Well...maybe I could come in for a few hours one day..."

"How about every day?"

Her eyes widened. "What?"

"A few hours every day. A part-time situation."

She shook her head, exasperated with him again. So this was his great idea. "Carter, you know that's impossible."

"You keep saying everything is impossible."

"Because it is." She took a deep breath and thought for a moment. "All right. I'll be in tomorrow morning. But just for a few hours. And just this once."

"Pendleton..."

"That's all, Carter. I'll see you in the morning."

Chapter Four

Morning didn't seem to mean eight o'clock to Pendleton anymore. Carter was in early, but there was no sign of his former associate. He spent a lot of time trying to concentrate on his work but looking up at every odd sound or movement and getting nothing done.

It was almost eleven before she came rushing in from the elevator. He'd never seen her looking so disheveled before. The first thing that occurred to him was that she'd been assaulted on her way to the office. She looked like she'd been in a train wreck. Every protective instinct he possessed came to life and he felt his adrenaline rising.

"What happened?" Carter asked, vaulting from his chair and moving out to greet Amy with some alarm. "Are you okay?"

"Me?" She gazed at him distractedly, pushing hair back out of her eyes. "Sure. Why do you ask?" But she didn't wait for an answer.

Looking around the office as though she hadn't seen it in a long, long time, she spoke, her words distinct but hurried. "Where are the problems you want me to tackle? I have to hurry. I only have the sitter for three hours."

"Pendleton." He gazed at her, appalled.

Her usual professional look and manner was strangely missing. Stray hairs were already escaping from the twist at the back of her neck, and a long strand was falling down over her eyes. One tail of her blouse was working its way out of the waistband of her wrinkled skirt, her hem was drooping, both legs of her panty hose had runs, and...

"Pendleton, I hate to point this out at a time like this, but your shoes don't match."

"What?" She looked down. "Yes, they do."

"Come here and look at them in the light. You see? One is black and the other is navy blue."

"Oh." She looked up at him, exasperated. "Oh, who cares? Do you really think that's a problem?" She threw up her hands. "Mister, you don't know problems. Try having your dishwasher flood the kitchen with soapsuds just as you hear the trash collector coming down the street and you realize you haven't put the trash cans out and the eighteen-month-old child has locked herself in the bathroom and the phone is ringing…'' She closed her eyes for just a moment and shuddered.

"I take it all these things happened to you this morning," he said calmly, trying not to laugh. Somehow he knew one snicker at a time such as this might tarnish their relationship forever.

"Oh, yes," she said. "That and much, much more." Her eyes took on a wild look he'd never seen in them before. "So you see, I don't have time to deal with trivialities like mismatched shoes. Just be glad I didn't arrive barefoot." She waved a hand at him. "Don't you understand? There are larger issues in life."

He kept his tongue firmly in his cheek. "Such as trash flow management," he murmured.

"Exactly." She studied his gaze sharply, as though looking for any hint that he might be making fun of her. "Let's get down to business, shall we? I only have a short time for this."

"You said that you would give me half a day," he reminded her.

"A half a day? Ha! I don't even know what day it *is*. A half a day." She looked around. "You have missing files? I'll find them. Just tell me what you want."

"Okay, but we also need some things translated."

"Give them to me and I'll call in the translation from home."

"Home?" He wasn't sure why, but it annoyed him to have her call it that.

"Yes. Meg's house is my home for the duration."
She met his gaze defiantly. "So where are the problems?"

He showed her and she got to work, moving like a whirlwind. She spent exactly two and a half hours at the office but she did clear up a lot of work that had been left undone. It was strange how good she looked to him, even in the uncharacteristically untidy state she was in. After all, it had only been three days since they'd parted at the hospital. That was hardly enough time to begin missing someone. And yet he found himself watching every move she made almost hungrily, enjoying having her around.

He resented it when the projects manager showed up for a prearranged meeting and he had to shut his office door and thereby shut off his view of her. But he managed not to let his annoyance show. It would have been a little too embarrassing if anyone noticed how he drank in every sight of her and waited to hear her voice. He wasn't even sure himself just why he was reacting this way. The last thing in the world he wanted to do was to analyze it.

Amy felt a sense of relief when his office door was shut. She knew he was watching her in a way he never had before and it was making her very nervous. But she was being torn by so many conflicting thoughts and new emotions, his scrutiny was just another factor in her ongoing ennui.

She loved being back in the office—and hated it at the same time. It wasn't hers any longer, and yet she felt so in control when she was here—something she wasn't feeling in her child-care role. She missed it, but at the same time, she couldn't throw herself into it completely as half her mind was always back at Meg's house with the children, wondering if all was going well there, wondering if she should call to check up on the baby-sitter, wondering if the baby was being too fussy for the sitter to handle.

She met Martha and showed her a few tricks of the trade, was greeted by others from the various offices like a long lost friend, and was generally made to feel very much as though she'd come back where she belonged.

"Boy, do we ever miss you," Delia admitted to her as they went over a list of address changes that needed updating. "All the unattached women in this company have been circling Carter like hungry wolves since they heard you were gone."

Amy looked at her in surprise. "But Carter and I weren't an item. Not ever. We weren't even dating."

"That's true," Delia said, looking at her wisely over her glasses. "But there was always an aura around the two of you. You were a team and it showed. That kept most of the flirting down to a dull roar."

Amy shrugged. "Well, let them take their chances with him. History suggests they won't get any further than I did."

She looked at the older woman curiously. Delia

had worked for Carter for years, yet Amy had never asked her much about the past before. She leaned forward and gazed at her with a speculative glint in her eyes.

"Have you ever, in all your time with him, known him to fall head over heels in love?" she asked her.

Delia thought for a moment, then slowly shook her head. "He used to date a lot more in the old days," she noted. "But there never seemed to be anyone special. Not that I noticed, anyway."

They went back to editing the list, but her words stayed with Amy. For some reason, she couldn't get them out of her mind.

Carter came out of his office just before she left. She looked at him and something emotional rose in her throat. She might not see him again for a long time. Suddenly she had the urge to embrace him— just a friendly goodbye. But she paused and once the impulse faded, she knew it was hopeless. Carter was not a hugger.

"I guess I'll see you…" Her voice trailed off because she really couldn't promise another session and so there was no point in promising anything.

"Sooner rather than later, I hope," he said smoothly. Then a faint smile curved his lips, as though he thought he had an ace in the hole or something similar. One eyebrow rose. "We have a situation I haven't briefed you on yet."

"Carter…" She began backing toward the elevator.

"Pendleton," he countered, throwing out an arm and leaning against the wall in a way that blocked her progress. "This is important. Something only you can help with."

She looked up into his eyes. They were standing very close, much closer than they usually got, and she was suddenly very much aware of his eyelashes. Why that made her heart begin to beat in a new and very provocative rhythm, she wasn't sure. But it did, and she had to work harder than usual to remember to be firm with him.

"I don't work here anymore. You keep forgetting that."

"The Joliet Aire negotiations are what I'm referring to," he went on, ignoring her retort. "We're setting up a conference call for tonight. Monsieur Jobert will be expecting to speak to you, I'm sure."

Her heart gave a leap. She couldn't help it. Old habits died hard. What a coup that would be—to land the contract for a large French resort. She'd talked to Mr. Jobert endlessly while they were in Paris, charming and cajoling him, but he'd stayed very noncommittal and she hadn't been able to tell if she was getting anywhere.

If he was still interested… But that wasn't her business any longer. Carter would have to manage things on his own. Still, she couldn't help but feel a pang.

She managed to keep from letting it show and she glared at Carter. "I won't be available to speak to him,'' she said crisply. ''I'm sure you'll make my excuses. He'll have to understand.''

Reaching out, she pushed Carter's arm out of her way. Something in his gaze made her catch her breath, but she didn't let it stop her. Giving him a quick but fleeting smile, she turned on her heel, and headed for the exit.

He watched her leave and he swore softly under his breath. This wasn't going to work—this letting her quit business. The moment she stepped onto the elevator, the lights seemed to dim, the background music seemed annoying and the excitement went out of the day. She had to come back to work for him, and it had to be soon. There was just no other option. Nothing worked right when Pendleton wasn't there.

What the hell—he might as well admit it. He just needed her too damn much.

By the following morning, he decided he'd been acting like a wounded dog and it was time to move on. Pendleton wasn't the only woman in the world. He was going to have to figure out a way to get through the rest of his life without her.

Monsieur Jobert had not been pleased to have Carter to deal with. They had tried foisting Martha on him, but that hadn't worked any better than Carter had thought it would. The French resort might be a lost cause.

What the hell. So be it. He could not waste any more of his energies mooning over an old employee.

By noon, he realized he was spending more time and effort trying to keep himself from picking up the phone and calling Pendleton than he was on his work. By afternoon, he'd had calls from two board members, both emphasizing how important the French project would be to his future with the company. Mrs. Leghorn had been especially caustic. By late afternoon, he'd decided he had to make one more attempt to get Pendleton back. There was just no denying that he needed her—both personally and professionally.

"Might as well face it," he muttered to himself. But that wasn't dejection he was feeling. More like anticipation.

He left work early and went straight out to Meg's place. He'd never been there before but he had no trouble finding it. The house was a charming little Craftsman cottage with a long front porch and windows with beautifully beveled panes. The front door was ajar and as he walked up on the porch, he could hear a baby crying and two children squabbling. And then there was Pendleton's voice, a little too carefully controlled, a little too patient, as though she was remaining so at great cost to her sanity.

"Scamp. Deedee. Please come here. Please, children. I can't leave the baby. Please come in here."

He thought he could detect the edge of hysteria, but maybe he was overstating the case a little.

Smiling grimly, he entered the house and made his way into the family room where the two youngsters were both pulling on a small toy piano and yelling at each other.

"Hey," he said. "Watch out. Someone's going to get hurt."

Their heads whipped around and both mouths dropped open. Forgotten, the little piano fell to the floor with a crash as they both turned and ran to where, he assumed, Pendleton must be.

"Aun' Amy, Aun' Amy! There's a man here!"

"A man?"

Carter found her in the baby's room, holding the baby on the changing table with one hand while she reached for a clean diaper with another. Only a couple of strands of hair still clung to the scrunchee at the back of her neck. The rest flew around her face in a storm of blond confusion. Was it his imagination, or were her beautiful eyes filled with desperation?

"Carter!" she cried once she saw him. "What are you doing here?"

"Looking for you."

"I'm…I'm in the middle of diapering this baby and I'm…I'm—"

She was having problems. That much was evident. The baby was kicking and twisting and generally making things difficult. There was a diaper pushed out of the way on the floor—obviously a failed attempt that had been dropped and discarded.

In reaching for a new one, Amy had knocked over the pad that held the pins, which now fell clattering to the floor.

Carter took in the situation in a glance, walked right up and took over.

"Okay, Pendleton," he said as he picked up the diaper pins. "You take care of those two kids for a minute. I'll handle the diaper."

And he picked a clean one off the stack, lifted the baby by her tiny little feet and slipped the diaper expertly beneath her baby bottom before deftly pinning the first side in a very professional-looking tuck.

Amy gaped at him. "What are you doing?" she squeaked.

"Putting on a diaper," he responded, finishing the job and swinging the baby up against his shoulder with expertise.

Amy shook her head, still not sure what she was seeing. "Where did you learn to do that?"

"I grew up in a very large family," he said nonchalantly.

He gave the baby a couple of pats, then swung her down into the bassinet. Scamp and Deedee were staring at him, as well, as though they didn't believe what they were witnessing any more than Amy did.

"You learn these things," he told her. "It's like riding a bicycle. You don't forget how to do it, no matter how hard you try."

Carter diapering a baby. Carter taking care of

children. No, the picture didn't work for her, even though she'd seen it with her own eyes. Carter wore silk Italian suits and had his newspaper delivered by courier and vacationed on the French Riviera. Carter didn't do child care. It just wasn't possible. She sank into a handy chair, suddenly too weary to stand any longer.

She closed her eyes. She was just so tired. This was it. She'd gone over the edge. Maybe she was delirious. Maybe Carter wasn't even in the room and she was dreaming...

But he had to be here, because now he was lifting her up, one arm under her knees, another around her shoulders, supporting her back.

"Hey," she said groggily, blinking up into his face. "What do you think you're doing?"

"You are going to take a nap," he told her firmly. "Which way to her bedroom, kids?"

"A nap!" She slipped her arms around his neck and clung to him as he carried her through the house. He felt so strong and smelled so good, she was tempted to close her eyes and press her face to his neck. But she couldn't do that. This was Carter!

"My mother took a nap every day," he told her as he kicked open the door to Meg's bedroom, where Amy was sleeping these days. "She swore by them."

A nap. What a crazy idea. And yet, what a seductively delicious idea. To sleep! She thought she remembered what that was—something she used to do in the old days, before she'd taken charge of all these moppets. Something it seemed you didn't get to do any more once you were a mother.

"But who took care of the children when your mother took a nap?" she asked him worriedly.

"The older ones took care of the younger ones." He dropped her gently onto the bed and pulled back the covers for her. "Just consider me the oldest kid around," he told her with a smile. "I'll take care of everything, including the baby. And you get to sleep."

Looking up into his eyes, she saw something she had never seen before. She struggled to identify what it was, but somehow it eluded her. She only knew he was making her feel very small and young and protected, and now, very safe.

And yet, should she? Was this just more delusional thinking on her part? And was it okay that she was doing this?

She was too tired to make decisions. Carter was making decisions for her, and she was willing to let him at this point. He pulled the drapes to darken the atmosphere, and she lay right where he'd put her, only dimly aware of him leaving the room, of Deedee and Scamp following him, their eyes intensely interested.

Her own eyes were drifting blessedly shut when she heard the scrabbling sound that told her Fred was probably under her bed.

"Okay, Fred," she whispered sleepily. "I've got no time for you now. Catch ya later."

And she sank into a deep sleep.

She woke up hours later. The house was eerily quiet. She lay there for a few minutes reorienting herself, trying to remember why she was in Meg's bed in Meg's bedroom. As memory returned, she realized it was just too quiet. She couldn't even hear any sign of Fred. She hadn't heard quiet like this since she'd lived alone.

In fact, it was too darn quiet. She rolled out of bed and pulled herself together, then raced into the main area of the house, her heart in her throat. She shouldn't have slept! What had she been thinking? She'd left her charges alone with a man who was, to them, a stranger. How could she have done such a thing? Was she crazy?

She skidded on the polished wood floor at the opening to the family room and came to a stop in front of the couch. There was Carter, reading a magazine, looking very in control and peaceful. He looked up and smiled at her.

"Hey, Goldilocks," he said, the area around his eyes crinkling with amusement.

"The children—" she began anxiously, her gaze darting around the room, looking for any signs of them.

"Asleep," he interjected, stopping her cold.

She blinked at him. "But…but they need to eat," she said, glancing at the clock on the mantel.

"They've eaten," he said calmly, enjoying the sight of her, so sleepy and rumpled-looking. Her hair was a tangled web of silver-blond around her pretty face, and her eyes were heavy-lidded. He'd never seen her look sexier. He put down the magazine, trying not to notice how lovely her breasts looked under the soft jersey shirt, how long and slim her bare legs looked in the running shorts she wore.

"We saved some for you."

Rising from the couch, he led her into the dining room. A covered plate sat waiting along with a place setting and a glass of water. Removing the cover with a flourish, Carter revealed an apple-and-shrimp salad nicely presented in a china bowl. A buttered dinner roll sat alongside.

She stared at the meal, then looked at him blearily, thrown completely off guard and still feeling as though she might be half asleep.

"I don't understand," she said, pushing hair out of her eyes. "What's happened?"

"Well, you've been asleep for four hours. During that time I've been taking care of the kids. I got them fed and put to bed. I made you something to eat. That's about it."

"But…" She looked around at the serene scene, the nicely prepared food, the tidiness of it all. It should have made her feel wonderful, comforted, secure. Instead, she felt devastated by it. Her defenses were down and her emotions were running wild. She tried to hold back, but she couldn't. Her face crumpled a bit and her lower lip began to tremble.

"Why is it that you can do such a good job of this so easily while I—I..."

"Stop," he told her firmly, barely resisting the impulse to reach out and take her chin in his hand. "You've been working around the clock at this for days. I've only been here for four hours."

He smiled at her. "I wouldn't be able to stand up to the strain for four days, either. Three young kids are too much for any one person full-time—especially someone who has no experience at it." He gestured. "Sit down and eat something."

She sank into the chair but she wasn't sure she was going to be able to eat. "Maybe I should go check on the children," she said fretfully, starting to get back up.

"No." He touched her shoulder, making her sit back down, but immediately withdrew his hand. "Trust me. They are fine and sound asleep. You'll only risk waking them again."

That was certainly something she didn't want to do. She'd learned very quickly that a sleeping child was something to be treasured.

And she did trust him, she realized as she looked up at his handsome face. That was something she could count on. Settling back in her chair, she picked up a fork and stabbed at a piece of shrimp, then watched as Carter sank into a chair across from her.

"Why are you doing this?" she asked him softly.

His smile was nonchalant. "There wasn't much choice. You were dead on your feet."

She stared at him for a moment, then went back to eating. She knew it was more than that. He was the one who was always talking about hiring people to do things. It would have been more in character for him to pull out his cell phone and hire a mother's helper for her, right on the spot. Taking over and doing these things himself—it just didn't fit the image.

But maybe she had the wrong image.

Or maybe it was something else. She frowned, chewing on a piece of crisp apple. Maybe he really wanted something from her. Now that would be more like the Carter James she knew. She looked at him sharply, wondering what it could be.

And he looked right back, challenging her with his brilliant gaze.

She gave him the ghost of a smile and went back to eating.

Carter's eyes darkened and his long fingers began playing with a stray silver spoon, turning it against the floral pattern in the linen tablecloth. It was all very well to win a few verbal exchanges, but he knew he was needlessly flirting with danger here. It was one thing to vaguely feel attracted at the office. It was another to be here with this sleepy, sexy woman, knowing there was a bed very near. That put a whole new perspective on things.

He remembered how she'd felt when he'd carried her into the bedroom, soft and silky, warm and breathing—how she'd looked as he'd laid her down on the plush bedding. Something twisted inside him and he looked away.

It was the same old thing. He'd been attracted to her from the first. The first day she'd walked into his office his libido had stirred, and he'd known, if he hired her, he'd have to be extra careful. He'd always been on alert around the women who worked for him, but from the first, there had been something special about her. He'd known she would take circumspect handling. Mixing business with pleasure was never a good idea. It always led to grief.

She finished eating and sat back with a sigh. She was beginning to feel downright human after all.

"That was delicious," she told him, her eyes sparkling. "I didn't know you were so handy with a kitchen."

"I've got talents you've never dreamed of," he said smoothly. "Someday you'll learn not to sell me short."

Her gaze caught his for just a moment, and she found herself smiling at him.

"I have nothing but respect for you," she said lightly. "But who would have ever thought you would be so good at diapering babies?"

He shrugged as though it were perfectly natural.

"It wasn't one of those things I bragged to my buddies about when I was younger," he admitted. "But I was considered pretty accomplished with a diaper in my day. I had to be. I had five younger brothers and sisters to help take care of."

She laughed softly, enjoying the way his eyes glittered in the lamplight. "You certainly have me beat," she said. "Those diaper pins are my undoing. I just can't get the hang of them." She made a face. "Actually, I was thinking about getting some disposables from the store. I hear they're easier to use."

"Amateur," he scoffed. "I'll show you the secret techniques. Once you get the hang of it…"

"It's like riding a bicycle," she said, laughing at him. "Yes, someone already said that."

She sobered, contemplating how the day had gone. He was right. She had been at the end of her rope. What might have happened if he hadn't shown up when he had? She hated to think of the possibilities. When you let yourself get that tired, bad decisions were just asking to be made.

She looked at him, sitting there across the table, looking so cool and crisp and sure of himself. She remembered feeling more like that herself. In the business world, she knew what she was doing. Here…she didn't. Her eyes clouded.

"Carter?" she asked softly. "Why am I failing at this?"

Chapter Five

Carter gave a dismissive grimace and leaned forward.

"You're not failing at this," he said sternly. "All in all, you've been doing a damn good job. You're just overwhelmed at times, and I caught you at one of those times."

She thought about that for a moment, not sure she bought it. But she knew one thing. Carter had been a lifesaver today.

She rose to take her plate to the kitchen and he rose with her. Suddenly she turned, wanting to thank him, wishing she could think of a way of doing it that he could appreciate. She knew he wasn't a hugger. She knew he avoided touching her most of the time. But she was a tactile person and she was itching to throw her arms around him and...

"Carter," she said, smiling at him, eyes shining. "Thank you."

Before he could say anything she made her move, reaching up to kiss him on one cheek while her right hand caressed the other.

"Today you have been a true friend," she added as she pulled back. "I think you must be my very best friend."

He stood like stone staring down at her. "I'm not a friend," he said gruffly, his eyes unreadable. "I'm your boss."

She searched his gaze for any hint of humor, but couldn't find any evidence of it. He meant it. Throwing up her hands, she laughed as she turned and reached out to take her plate. But something inside her almost felt like crying.

He followed her into the kitchen, which was spotless. She knew he must have been working here, as well, because she remembered leaving it in a very messy state just a few hours before. She turned toward him, her delight in the state of the kitchen written on her face, and he backed away, holding his hands up as though to defend himself.

"No more kissing," he warned, eyes hooded. "You don't kiss the boss."

"*I* do," she noted, laughing again. But she didn't try to force it on him. "Oh, Carter. You're just like the little elves that come in the night. You want no thanks or recognition. You toil in anonymity."

"Hardly that," he said dryly, but finally a spark of amusement was allowed to show.

"True. You've never been one to hide your light under a bushel," she teased. "So this must be a part of some larger agenda."

He turned away, but just before he did, she saw something flash across his face and she realized she must have hit home with her remark. Well, that was hardly surprising. She'd known all along he hadn't just dropped by for a friendly chat.

As she ran water over her dishes, she contemplated confronting him about it, then rejected the idea. He would tell her in his own good time. She was pretty sure it had something to do with the office. He was going to try to talk her into coming back. Well, he might as well save his breath on that one.

"Hey, you've got a great patio back here." Carter had been exploring and opened the kitchen door to the patio, stepping out and gazing around. "You can see stars and hear the ocean." He peered back in at her. "How about having a glass of wine out here, where we can talk?"

"Well, that didn't take long," she murmured to herself, reaching for the bottle on the counter and two wineglasses.

"What?"

"Nothing." She chuckled as she went out to join him. "Oh, Carter, you just don't understand that I know you so well, do you?" she whispered to herself. "Unfortunately, the light doesn't seem to work," she noted out loud after she'd tried it.

"No problem," he countered. "There's enough moon to see by."

Just barely. But Carter took the bottle from her and filled the glasses as she pulled two chairs up beside a small fishpond edged with ferns and primroses, just illuminated by the light from the door to the kitchen they'd left open so that they could hear if any of the children called out. They sat side by side in the moonlight and watched the stars ride across the sky and listened to the ocean, a good three or four blocks away, as it beat itself silly against the shore.

Very quickly, the conversation got back to what Amy felt was her failure as a child-care provider. That was what was on her mind. But Carter tried to make excuses for her.

"This was an insane thing for you to undertake," he lectured, waving his wineglass in the night air. "You should never have done it. You should have hired somebody right from the first."

"Oh, you keep saying that, but you just don't understand," she said wistfully. "I *wanted* to do this for my sister. I needed to do it."

"Really? So you are really undergoing this torture for your own good, somehow."

He was scoffing at what she'd told him. She contemplated the golden liquid in her glass and thought of how she could explain this to him.

"It's just that, where Meg is concerned, I feel so guilty," she said.

"Guilty? Where do you have any guilt in this matter?"

She turned toward him in the chair. "You know very well that, other than my job, I've had no life for a good long time."

He shrugged. "You and me both," he commented softly.

"Yes, I know." She made a face at him. "But right now we're talking about me."

His eyes brimmed with amusement. "Oh, it's always all about you, isn't it, Pendleton?"

She threw him a quelling look and went on as though he hadn't teased her. "When I look back over the years, I have to admit I've been a lousy sister to Meg. Where was I when she and Tim exchanged wedding vows? I was delivering papers to a surveying company in Japan. Where was I when Scamp was born? A good sister would have been there, ready to help her make the adjustment to becoming a mom, but I was on a fact-finding mission in Thailand. When Deedee was born, I was working for you. Remember? We got stuck in a snowstorm in Finland and couldn't get out for two days."

"Act of God," he murmured. "Couldn't be helped."

"When Jillian was born I was in Paris delivering the final papers on the Amherst deal. But the point is, I was always too busy. I was always all wrapped up in myself and my career. I haven't been there for her once.'' She sighed, the guilt drowning her again. ''So this time, I'm bound and determined to do what I can to help her. No matter what.''

''Very commendable,'' he said. ''I'm going to have to work on ways to make you feel guilty about me. Then I can obviously get you to do whatever I want you to do.''

She groaned, knowing he still didn't get it.

''How are Meg and Tim doing, by the way?'' he asked before she could try to explain further.

''They seem to be coming along fairly well, according to the doctors.'' She brightened as she remembered something. ''I actually got to talk to Meg on the telephone for a few minutes today. That was a big step, I think. She sounded very, very tired.''

''Probably on pain medication.''

''Oh, of course. But she was pretty lucid and she's full of determination to get back to her kids as quickly as possible.''

''Good.''

''I put each one of the kids on and let them say hi to her. Even the baby.''

She could see his smile in the dim light. ''No wonder they were a little on the hyper side.''

She cocked her head toward him, considering. ''You think?''

''Sure. That's what kids do. Good things, bad things, anything a little out of the ordinary will upset their emotional equilibrium and the way they express that is through making life miserable for adults." He grinned again. "That's the best time to put them down for naps."

She stared at him in wonder. "I can't believe you know so much about these things."

"I know this." He fixed her with a stern look. "You're trying to be a hero, doing it all on your own, and there is no reason for it. Hire someone to help you, at least."

She shook her head, being stubborn. "I've got to do this myself. Didn't I just explain to you? And anyway, I wouldn't know what to do or how to go about finding someone I could trust."

"That's not so hard."

"Really." She threw him an exasperated look. "You make everything sound so easy. But you're not the one who has to do it. Or to be responsible once you do."

He didn't respond and for a long moment they sat in silence, listening to the sounds of nature mixed with cars on the highway not too far away. The faint strains from a neighbor's sound system hinted at a Rachmaninoff concerto. The soft night and the effects of the wine were beginning to take their toll on Amy, and when she sensed that Carter had turned his head and was looking at her, her pulse quickened.

If only Carter were the romantic sort, she thought wistfully. This was the perfect setting for a little flirtation. And she could easily be put in the mood.

Their chairs were close together. She could almost hear him breathing. What if she were to turn right now and look deeply into his eyes? Would he finally see that she could be more to him than a business partner?

"Pendleton."

She jumped, jolted out of her dream. Turning, she met his gaze, but somehow that connection didn't have the electricity she'd been hoping for.

"Pendleton, I've got an idea for you."

She blinked at him and sighed. She was pretty sure his idea wasn't going to have anything to do with cool starlit nights and hot kisses on the patio. "What is it?"

He leaned forward. "It's more of a bargain, really. I think I can help you with all your problems. And at the same time, you can help me."

Amy stared at him. "Really? And how are we going to do this marvelous thing?"

"It's the old barter system. We both win if we play it right."

She sighed. Whom did he think he was fooling, anyway? "Okay. I'll bite. I know you want me to come into the office a few hours every day. Which I can't do. But I'm sure that's my side of the bargain. What's yours?"

He sat back as though appalled that she would think his idea might be so crass. "That's not it at all. I understand completely that you can't come into the office. You've made that perfectly clear."

"You're kidding. You're actually going to accept that?"

"Of course. I don't want you to come into the office at all." He smiled at her. "We can do everything right here."

She gazed at him skeptically. "What are you talking about? You've got a job. You can't just walk out and come help me."

His smile was mysteriously secretive. "I can do what I damn well please as long as I get results, and you know it." He emptied his wineglass and reached for a refill. "Now here's the deal. We'll do it as a trade. You help me out on the Joliet Aire project and I'll help you with the kids."

She stared at him for a moment. "You've said that every which way but clearly. Just exactly how do you mean to do this?"

"We'll do it right here. I can make calls from here as well as from my office. You can make some, too. You can go over letters, make contacts, while I give you some relief from the child care. If I'm here, you will have time to run over to the hospital to see your sister. You can go out and do some errands without having to drag the kids along. I can make your life so much easier, just by being around."

She shook her head, a smile barely touching her lips. "Oh, Carter, you are so crafty."

"It's a simple trade-off." He shrugged as though that should be evident to any casual observer.

"You never give up, do you?"

He sat back and took a sip of his wine. "That's the secret to my success." He waved a hand at her. "This is something I really need. And I'm willing to offer you something you really need in exchange. What could be more business-like than that?"

She thought it over. What would it hurt if he came over for a couple of hours a day? She would make a few phone calls for him, set up a couple of meetings, put together a few reports, and he would give her some help with the children. Why not? It would actually be a relief to her to have a respite occasionally. And he had certainly proved that he could take over where the children were concerned.

She was tempted to say yes.

Still, as she sat talking with him, sipping the glass of wine he'd poured for her, relaxing, feeling like a human being again, one part of her mind was watching it all with a skeptical eye.

You thought you'd finally gotten away from him. You thought that this was just the first step in striking out on your own, that you were going to find someone to marry, settle down to a domestic life. You know very well, the longer you stay tied to Carter, the less chance you have of ever getting married and having children at all.

Do you really want to get married and have children? was the next thought. The past few days had certainly shaken that goal to its roots, Amy mused. That was a puzzle for another day, however.

She knew she was going to take him up on his

offer. Actually, it seemed a lifesaver to her at the moment. After all, she and Carter made an unbeatable team. Why not?

And yet she also knew that she was asking for more frustration if she did this. Carter kept his distance, and he kept the most distance just when she most yearned for contact. Still, she didn't have a whole lot of choice. And, she had to admit, she wouldn't mind getting away from the children to do a little business for a short period every day. That might help her feel like a full human being again.

"Okay," she said at last. "We'd better work out some ground rules first. And set up a schedule. But I guess it really would be for the best."

The next day started out as hectic as all the others, but for some reason she felt a little better able to cope. She was actually refreshed by her night's sleep, instead of feeling as if she were merely being kept alive. She found herself singing to baby Jillian as she changed her diaper, and the baby responded in kind, gurgling back at her, making her laugh.

She'd just outfitted Jillian in a clean playsuit and put her in the automatic swing and settled Deedee and Scamp down in front of the television for *Sesame Street* when the doorbell rang.

"Hmm," she murmured, glancing at the clock. It was awfully early. "Who could that be?"

Knuckles firmly knocked, to supplement the doorbell, before she made it to the door, and when she pulled it open, she was dumbfounded to find the front porch awash in workmen carrying large boxes or pushing carts or dollies filled with equipment. The men had a sturdy, dedicated look to them, as though they knew what had to be done and were ready to do it. She stared.

"Miss Amy Pendleton?" the first man read off a purchasing order. "I've got your office unit ready to install. If you'll just let me take a look at the room where you want this so I can prepare for installation..."

"I have no idea what you are talking about," Amy said, shaking her head and wishing it were the truth. "I didn't order an office unit." Though she had a very bad feeling she might know who had.

"Says right here, Amy Pendleton," he said, reading off the address. "That's you, right?"

Amy frowned. She was beginning to smell a rat. "You can put my name wherever you want, I didn't order it," she repeated. "And I'm not accepting delivery. Thank you just the same."

She began to push the door shut, but another man stepped forward and put his foot in the way.

"Excuse me, miss," he said around the stub of an unlit cigar. "But I've got this here computer you ordered. Where you want I should put it?"

"Will you please sign for this, Miss Pendleton?" a third man cried reedily, trying to elbow his way in between the others.

"What is it?" she asked him distractedly.

"Two reams of typing paper, one ream of fax paper, one ream of copy paper, two toner cartridges…"

"Where do you want this fax machine?" a fourth yelled, coming up the steps. "I've got twelve more rush deliveries to get done by nine o'clock, so I'd appreciate if you could…"

By now they were all yelling, at each other and at her, and she was fuming, denying, protesting, all to no avail. No one was listening.

Until a strange sound was heard and they all stopped for a moment to listen. Turning, they beheld Carter coming up the walk, his hands thrust into his trouser pockets, whistling a happy tune as he came strolling toward them in the morning sunlight, looking like a prosperous gentleman from an age gone by with barely any responsibilities and a lot of time to smell the roses.

"Good morning," he said as they all gaped at him. "Isn't it a beautiful day?"

"Carter!" Amy wailed, and at the same time every deliveryman started up again, this time aiming their complaints at Carter. He held up a hand for silence, and to Amy's surprise, he got it.

"One at a time," he said cheerfully.

"Me first," Amy demanded.

He hesitated, then graciously nodded toward her. "I suppose the woman of the house should have precedence," he admitted, looking to the men for understanding.

They grumbled and shuffled their feet, but they gave way, waiting to see what Amy had to say.

She took a deep breath. Now that she had her chance, she wasn't sure how she wanted to put this.

"Carter!" she said at last, crying out the only thing she could think of. "What have you done? What on earth is going on here?"

"I'm moving an office in, of course."

She opened her mouth, then closed it, then opened it again. "Who told you that you could do this?"

"But we have to do it. We can't do a decent job on the Joliet Aire account without the proper facilities." He said it slowly and calmly, as though talking to someone just a little thick.

"So you're putting in a whole new office." She threw up her hands. "Are you crazy?"

He looked taken aback, then turned to appeal to the men. "What do *you* think?" he asked, pretending innocence.

They all started to talk at once and he looked at Amy with a half smile, shrugging as though he had no control over them at all.

Amy looked at him standing there, sunlight in his hair, amusement hovering around his mouth and shining in his eyes. How could one man be so infuriating...and so delightful at the same time? She didn't know whether to laugh or to start yelling at him.

But this really was impossible. Utterly and completely impossible. How could he think he could just come in and take over this way? Her vision of him dropping by for a few hours a day and using the old computer in the den was beginning to fizzle.

"No, Carter," she said above the din, her eyes flashing. "You cannot move an entire office into Meg's house. You know very well I never gave permission for you to do any such thing."

He gazed at her in surprise—a surprise she had no doubt was feigned.

"But, Pendleton," he said innocently. "You agreed to do some work with me. We can't do that work without the proper tools. I'm just trying to make things easier for both of us. Surely you can understand that."

She swallowed, looking at the huge boxes these men were prepared to carry into the little house. "What exactly is all this?" she asked, her voice strained.

"Just the bare minimum." His casual wave in the direction of the equipment was meant to render it harmless—almost meaningless. "Things we need, like a fax machine, a computer with a fast Internet connection, a laser printer, a scanner, a—"

"Oh, Carter!" She was reeling. She had never dreamed he would do something like this. "How much time are you planning to spend here?"

He gave her his most charming grin. "Believe me, you'll hardly notice that I'm here at all."

She hardened her gaze and glared at him. "How

much of your day are you planning to spend here?"
she insisted once again.

"As much as it takes, of course. I'm a pragmatic
guy. I'll do what has to be done and that will be all.
You'll see."

Her frown wavered. There was something in the
way he said that… Why did she get the feeling that
he meant even more than the words implied? Still,
she knew she was losing the battle here. He did have
a point about needing these things. If she made him
take them all away again, she would end up back in
the situation she'd been in before. And she had to
admit, she didn't want that. He'd won her over. Or
beaten her back. It depended on how she looked at
it. Either way, in the end, she stood aside and let
the work proceed.

Carter gave her a dazzling smile that made her
want to whack him with something. He then began
directing the men to the den where he wanted everything put. He had it all worked out, it seemed,
including measurements.

"I didn't see you skulking around with a mea-
suring tape," she said accusingly. She stood with
her hands on her hips in the doorway of the den as
the workmen left, marveling at how everything had
been shoe-horned into place so easily. "When did
you do all this?"

He shrugged, going down on his knees to plug in
the power strip under a table. "While you were
sleeping."

"Long before you'd asked my permission," she pointed out grumpily. "Pretty cocky and sure of yourself, aren't you?"

He rose, dusting off the knees of his slacks. "Pendleton, after all the time we've spent together, I know you like I know the back of my hand."

"You know I'm a pushover, you mean," she muttered, crossing her arms at her chest, feeling surly.

"Hardly that." He looked shocked at the concept. "I had to do a lot of planning to persuade you to see things my way."

She turned and gave him a defiant look. "Now that's where you're wrong. I never did see things your way. I'm just…just accommodating your way for the time being." She wagged a finger at him, only half in jest. "You're on probation. I could kick you out at any moment."

He frowned thoughtfully, pretending to take her seriously, though his eyes were flirting in a way she liked a lot.

"Just so I know, what would you consider grounds for kicking me out?" he asked, pretending to be worried.

Her chin rose, and she pouted a bit. "Oh, I don't know. Loud music and wild parties, I suppose."

He mused, hand to chin. "Nubile women?"

She pretended to consider. "That would depend."

"On what?" He grinned, eyes dancing. "On how naked they were?"

She couldn't keep back the laugh at that one.

"Yes, that would be a consideration," she admitted. "Let's just say no naked women and leave it at that."

"Spoilsport. But I'll make a note of it."

"See that you do."

They were standing very close and she could see in his eyes that he knew they were treading dangerously close to an actual flirtation. But she could also see that he was enjoying it, that he didn't want to pull away just yet. And that gave her a surge of excitement the likes of which she hadn't felt in a good long time.

Still, another part of her, the part that had all the good sense, was warning her not to build any hope from this.

The man doesn't want to be intimate with you, her good sense reminded her. *Even when he's tempted, he keeps an iron control over his reactions. So don't harbor any silly dreams. He's your boss. Remember? And he doesn't want to be any more than that.*

Chapter Six

"The first thing you'd better do," Carter said as he gazed around his new office with a look of satisfaction on his handsome face, "is go visit your sister at the hospital."

Go off on an excursion all by herself? Amy suddenly realized that over the past five days, she'd only done that once, and that was when she'd gone in to work. Everything else had been accomplished with the children glued to her legs or in her arms. But they were all down for naps and she had someone to look after them while she was gone.

"You know what?" she said with a sense of wonder. "I can stop at the grocery store. I haven't done that all week."

"Okay." He nodded, his attention diverted by

some problem with the wiring on the computer again. "I'll expect you back when you get back."

"Great." She hesitated, still a little wary of this whole arrangement. "Are you really sure you want to do this?"

"Of course."

He looked up at her and felt like chuckling. She really had no idea. He had no qualms about taking care of the children. He'd always had a knack for it, no matter how much he'd tried to suppress it over most of his life. He hadn't been around children of this age for almost twenty years, and yet the ability for dealing with them still seemed to be there. It all just worked. He didn't know how it happened. It just did. It always had. Why that was he had no idea, but he wasn't going to second guess it now when it was coming in mighty handy.

He looked into their eyes and they looked into his and something went snap and something inside him said, Yes. I can handle this.

"Wasn't I okay last night?" he asked her.

"Yes." A smile curled her lips.

He had been more than okay. And the children really seemed to like him. In fact, this morning they'd followed him around as if he were the Pied Piper, interested in everything he said and did. It was kind of cute. She only wished they could bond to her as easily.

That first night they had clung to her, but she realized now they had been scared and worried

about their parents and it had been a case of knowing she was their aunt and therefore the one to go
to for comfort and protection. Since then, they'd
seemed a lot less interested. It wasn't that they rejected her. Nothing as blatant as that. They seemed
to like her just fine. But they didn't adore her the
way they'd seemed to adore Carter right from the
first.

Maybe I'm just no good with kids.

That thought had come to her, but she'd pushed
it away. There was no point getting maudlin. Things
were working out quite well and she was getting
better at dealing with them every day.

She couldn't help but wonder, though, if having
her own would be just like this. And if so, did she
really want it? It did seem like an awful lot of drudgery. To be in charge of someone's well-being day
and night for years and years—could she handle it?
And did she really want to? The answers weren't as
clear cut as they had seemed only days ago.

"All right. I'll go," she said, gathering her purse
and her keys.

She was just about to make good on her promise
when the sound of footsteps told her someone was
approaching the front door. In a moment, someone
called through the screen.

"Hello! Anybody home?"

"Oh, it's Paul," she told Carter quickly. "The
neighbor Meg is always trying to fix me up with."
She gave a short laugh and turned.

One of Carter's eyebrows shot up, but she hardly noticed as she hurried to the front door. There stood Paul, looking inoffensive and pleasant, as usual.

"You're back from your sales trip."

Paul nodded, smiling at her. "Back, and so sorry to have left you in the lurch as it were. I've brought a peace offering to make up for it." He held up a plate of cookies. "Shortbread cookies," he told her with a rather goofy grin. "I baked them just for you."

"Why, Paul, how nice of you!" She was genuinely touched.

As she reached to take the plate of golden crisps from him she realized his expression had changed and she turned to see that Carter had come up behind her.

"Oh, hello," Paul said, his eyes exhibiting a sort of deer-caught-in-headlights aspect. "I—I didn't realize you had a friend here with you."

Amy glanced sideways at Carter and smiled. "Oh, no. Carter isn't a friend." She gave him an arch look. "Carter's my boss. Big difference."

"Oh, I see." Paul looked relieved to hear it. "Well, how do you do, Carter?" He stuck out a hand, which Carter shook with obvious reluctance. Something about the look on his face told everyone present that he was not prepared to become bosom buddies with this neighbor person.

"Carter has just moved an office in so that we

can get some work done and I can still care for the children,'' Amy explained.

''So he'll be staying here with you?'' Paul tried to seem unconcerned about the prospect, but failed miserably. A worried frown wrinkled his ample forehead and his gaze darted from one of them to the other as though he was trying to catch the truth on the fly.

''Only occasionally,'' Amy said quickly with a sly look at Carter's darkening brow. ''It's entirely a working relationship.''

''Well, I guess we'll be crossing paths from time to time,'' Paul said, making a much more successful attempt to seem friendly than Carter was making.

They stared at one another for a long moment, while Amy fidgeted, trying to think of something to say.

Then Paul turned, gazing around the area. ''Right now I'm looking for my cat. Pooky seems to be spending an inordinate amount of time skulking about in your sister's yard lately.''

''Really?'' Amy leaned out and made a quick survey of what she could see of the yard but didn't spot any sign of the huge tiger-striped animal. ''Have you tried calling him?''

''Exactly my plan,'' he said pleasantly. He waved at the two of them as he stepped back off the porch. ''Nice to have met you, Carter. Hope you get a lot of work done.''

Carter muttered something that might have

sounded like "You, too," or might have been something more offensive, but Amy really couldn't be sure.

"Thanks so much for the cookies," Amy called after him, and in just another moment he could be heard, calling, "Pooky! Pooky! Come here, you old furrmeister."

Carter turned slowly to face her. "What grown man names his cat Pooky?" he asked, a look of incredulity on his face.

Amy shushed him and softly closed the door. "Well, what would you name him?" she asked as she began getting her things together again, preparing to head out into the world.

"Tiger." He leaned against the doorjamb, thinking. "Or Rover."

"Rover is a dog's name." She flashed him a warning glance. "Cats are always named things like Muffy or Precious."

"No." He shook his head, obviously appalled. "Not my cats. I had a big black cat once. Named him Ninja. That's a great name for a cat." He grunted in disgust. "Pooky," he said again. "That's an insult to the cat world."

"Oh, get over it," she told him lightly. "Here, have a cookie. It'll make you happier."

He sneered at the plate she held toward him. "I wouldn't touch those with a ten-foot pole," he told her. "I make much better shortbread cookies than that."

She held back a grin. "You?" Shaking her head, she tried not to laugh. "I knew you'd been into gourmet cooking for years, but cookies?"

"You name it, I can cook it," he boasted. Looking at Paul's cookies, he made a face. "I doubt if this guy knows a sauté pan from a curling iron."

She turned to study him for a moment. It had suddenly occurred to her that there might be more to this grousing than met the eye. Could Carter possibly be...jealous? No, that really wasn't possible. But there was something in the air. She could feel it. And it made her smile.

Still, she didn't have time to think it over. She was about to fly solo for the first time in days and she was bound and determined to enjoy it.

"'Bye," she said, heading for the garage. *"Hasta la vista."*

Two hours later she was back, her arms full of groceries. She set the bags down on the kitchen table and went looking for her charges. There was no one in the family room, the living room, or the dining room, and the bedrooms were empty. That put her in the doorway of the den. She peeked in, not wanting to disturb Carter if he was working, and what she saw set her back on her heels.

There was the man himself taking a business call. He'd activated the speakerphone, which left his hands free. One hand was busy tickling Deedee's tummy as she wriggled on the floor at his feet, laughing uproariously. The other was rolling a ball to where Scamp sat, waiting to catch it and roll it back. Meanwhile, the baby was crawling around on a mat he'd set out in the corner of the room, gurgling happily and chewing on a rubber bunny toy. Complete chaos, and yet everything was working just fine.

Carter looked up when she came into the room and gave her a wink, but went on talking to Delia on the speakerphone. The children didn't even notice she was there.

It was an adorable scene. Standing there taking it all in, she wanted to love it. She really did.

But somehow, she just couldn't. Her first impulse was to complain, to carp, to ask him why he was letting the baby chew on that awful old toy, why he didn't stop Deedee's annoying laughter, why Scamp had a baseball cap on in the house. Luckily, she stopped herself in time, clamping her lips shut and turning away, leaving the room as quickly as she could. She was ashamed of her negativity, but she wanted to cry. Emotion clogged her thinking and she wasn't even sure why.

"Pendleton?"

He'd followed her out into the hallway. Taking a deep breath, she turned to greet him with the brightest smile she could muster.

"Is something wrong?" he asked her, looking concerned. "Your sister...?"

"Oh, no." She kept the smile going. "She is doing very well, actually. And she wants to talk to the children again this afternoon. So I mustn't forget to put in a call around three.''

He was frowning, searching her eyes. ''Then what is it?''

''Nothing. I'm just...tired, I guess.'' Her smile was beginning to feel painful and she began to let it fade. ''Will you be going into the office now that I'm back?'' she asked him.

He looked at her as though she'd asked something strange, or maybe he hadn't heard her right.

''Pendleton, this is my office now. I've got it all set up and I'm ready to roll. I might have to run downtown occasionally to look at some files or to attend a meeting, but for the most part, I'm set. I've got the phones hooked up, a direct line to Delia, Martha on call, and most importantly, you right here.'' He shrugged. ''I don't need to go back there.''

She stared at him. Of course. Was she so muddled in her thinking that she hadn't realized this when she saw all the equipment being moved in? Was she really getting so fuzzy she couldn't see reality when it stared her in the face? He'd moved in, lock, stock, and barrel, and she had stood by and let him.

A part of her was fuming. She really should do something about this. She should tell him no. This wasn't a part of their agreement. They had never been talking about more than a few hours a day. She was sure of it.

But her confidence was thrown off and she hesitated. Maybe what he was saying made a lot of sense. Maybe this was better than running back and forth, a few hours here, a few hours there. Maybe her feeling that he shouldn't be here so much had more to do with her resentment than it did with logic.

There. She'd been honest with herself. She felt resentment, darn it. That was what was upsetting her so. Why was this all so easy for him and so very hard for her? Why could he charm each one of the children with no effort at all, manage them, entertain them, and keep them in line, all while doing his job at the same time—and she practically turned herself inside out to do half as much and only muffed it every time. It wasn't fair!

The resentment burned inside her and made her wary of taking any steps she might regret. She wasn't going to confront him now. She would let him stay and watch how things went.

"Okay," she said, turning back to look at him. "That's fine."

She could see by the look in his eyes that he had expected more of a struggle. But he took her words with satisfaction and started back toward the den.

"I guess I'll get the children some lunch and put them down for naps," she said after taking a cleansing breath and attempting to calm herself down.

He paused and looked back. "I've already fed them," he said easily. "But you're right. They should go down for naps. Good timing. I've got to make some calls to Lima.''

She made a face at his back as he turned away again. "I'll bet you already did the dishes, too," she muttered, stomping into the kitchen and confirming her suspicions. "Probably while on the phone negotiating terms with the Hungarian ambassador.''

She glanced around for a likely pillow to scream into, but there wasn't one readily available so she skipped that bit of tension relief and went straight to work putting groceries away.

And then she saw the cookies. They were cooling on a rack on the far counter. Beautiful, golden, light and yet buttery-looking, they made her mouth water at first sight. Paul's looked pale and pitiful next to them. There was just no contest. And that was exactly the way Carter had planned it to be. She shook her head slowly, wondering what went on in that man's mind.

With a sigh, she turned away. It was time for the naps.

She put the baby down first, then went to gather the other two. She had to pry them away from Carter, which didn't help her disposition a whole lot. But once she got them out of the den, they came willingly enough and she managed to get into a good enough mood to sing them a nursery song while tucking them in.

They looked so adorable lying there in their little beds. An emotion she wasn't used to began to build in her chest. These children were precious to her. She wanted only good things to happen to them.

She leaned down to kiss Deedee, then went to Scamp and gave him a peck on the cheek, as well.

"Can Uncle Carter come kiss us good-night?" he asked in his high little-boy voice.

She froze. "It's not nighttime yet," she said lightly.

"But could he?"

She shook her head. "No, darling. Carter is much too busy right now. He has work to do."

She closed her eyes as she left the room, leaning back on the door. Why had she said that? That had been mean. But it was true. Carter had to get some work done and there was no real reason he should come racing up to kiss them now, after he'd already said goodbye to them a few minutes before. Still, she knew her motive for refusing them hadn't been pure and she felt rotten about it.

She went down to the den to find Carter poring through information on the Internet. "Need any help?" she asked, slumping down into a chair beside him.

He made a noncommittal noise without looking up and she sighed.

"I don't know if the kids should call you 'Uncle Carter,'" she said without preamble.

That got his attention. He reared back from the monitor screen and stared at her. "Why not?"

"Well, I'm the aunt. And if they call you the uncle, that implies certain things."

Her heart sank as she realized she was doing it again. She was picking a fight, and all because of pure resentment. What was the matter with her? She usually didn't do things like this. She hated that she was doing it now.

"I see," he said slowly. "You don't want anyone to get the wrong idea. You don't want anyone to assume we might be linked romantically."

"No, that's not what I mean at all."

Oh, how could she be so dumb? There was nothing she would like better than to be linked romantically with him. At least, she thought she would like it. If there turned out to be a future in it. If not...

"Pendleton, what is it? What has you so jumpy?" His eyes darkened and he moved closer. "What have I done?"

She blinked quickly to keep from tearing up. "Oh, Carter, you haven't done anything. It's all me."

And it was. She knew exactly what was bothering her. She'd watched him with the children and a little piece of her was jealous. She couldn't help it. They responded to him so naturally, as though they had always known—and loved—him. They adored him on sight. It was quite obvious. Even the baby quieted more quickly when he was the one to pick her up.

She was the aunt. She was the one related to them.

She was the one who had dedicated herself to their welfare. Why didn't they respond to her that way?

Taking a deep and shaky breath, she turned to face Carter and tried to explain, telling him as much as she could manage of how she felt and why. He listened without commenting, but he did shake his head now and then, and she could tell he thought she was being silly.

Well, of course she was being silly. She knew that. Emotions often made you say silly things. But that didn't make them any less valid. As she wound down her litany of woes, she felt a little embarrassed, but also pleased to have gotten it off her chest. And in the end, she asked him for help.

"What am I doing wrong?" she said simply.

She was afraid he would just tell her she was imagining things and turn back to the computer, hoping she would go away. But he didn't do that. Instead, he thought about it for a moment, his gaze traveling over her in a way that gave her shivers. But she knew he wasn't really looking at her. He was thinking. She had nothing to do with it.

"I think it must be because you're too uptight," Carter told her at last. "You're just too nervous. Kids can sense that sort of unease the way a dog can sense fear. You have to give them the feeling that you know what you're doing."

Amy groaned, letting her head fall back. "What if I *don't* know what I'm doing?"

"Fake it." His slow grin warmed the room.

"You're learning. It will come. You're getting better all the time."

She gave him a skeptical look. "How do you know?"

"I can see it." He smiled into her eyes. "Taking care of children is a natural thing. Treat it in a natural way. You'll do fine."

Their gazes held and a flash of wordless communication flared between them. *Natural. Yes, there was a lot of that natural stuff going around these days.*

At least, that was what she was thinking. But he seemed to have his mind on something else.

"Right now, for instance," he said, nodding at her. "Look at you. You look like you've got a coat hanger in your shirt. Relax. Loosen up. Here, let me try this."

He turned her in her swivel chair so that her back was to him and suddenly she felt his hands on her shoulders, kneading and rubbing.

She couldn't catch her breath. Carter was touching her and he was doing it voluntarily. Unbelievable. This had never happened before. The only other time they had had this much contact was when he'd carried her in for her nap the day before. Was this a trend? Oh, she surely hoped so!

As his strong fingers worked their way into the depths of her muscles, she felt her flesh begin to melt away. Her eyes closed dreamily.

"Oh." She sighed. "That feels so good."

"Just let go," he said softly as he worked. "Think about a cool mountain stream. Let every part of you relax."

Oooh, that would be dangerous.

Relaxing, letting nature take over—it all sounded very good, but she was afraid if she let herself do what came naturally, soon she would be reaching out for Carter and he might find himself fighting off more than a little kiss.

"How's that?" he asked, his voice so close to her ear.

"Wonderful," she whispered.

His touch was stirring a certain magic in her, awakening responses she hadn't heard from in a long time. His thumbs seemed to caress her spine while his fingers dug into her shoulders, sending a warm glow seeping throughout her body. His hands were so strong. Just like the rest of him. She thought about his long, lean body and his handsome face and then her heart was thudding so hard she was sure he must hear it. If she turned her head, would he pull away?

Probably. No, she had better just sit and let this heavenly massage go on for as long as he kept it up. The moment she turned to face him, he would back off. That was always the pattern.

"You've definitely loosened up," he said. "You feel good."

Good as in—the way he wanted her to relax? Or good as in—sexy? She didn't know and it was driving her crazy. Suddenly she wanted his kiss so badly, she couldn't stand it any longer. Throwing caution to the winds, she opened her eyes and turned her head.

His face was only inches away. His hands stopped moving, but he didn't pull them back. They sat on her shoulders, spreading heat from the center of his palms. She looked into his eyes and watched as his gaze dropped to her mouth. He was going to do it. She was sure. He was so near... She raised her face to his, her lips parting, waiting for him...

And then he was gone, rising out of the chair, acting business-like, as usual.

"Well, Pendleton," he said briskly, reaching for a stack of papers and shuffling through them as though he actually thought he was going to find something that way. "Enough of that for now. I've got work to do. And I'd like you to go over a couple of letters I've printed up, see if you can catch any flaws in my logic."

She turned in her chair, staring at him, heart still beating wildly, frustration burning in her soul. How could he have done this? Was he made of stone?

No. There had been a response in his eyes. She'd seen it, sensed it in his touch. He was purposefully trying to keep her at arm's length. And she'd had about enough of it.

"Carter," she said bluntly. "Why do you call me Pendleton?"

He stopped and looked down at her. "Isn't that your name?"

He tried to say it crisply, as though to prove nothing had been going on here, but they both knew better. And she wasn't going to let it fade away without demanding some sort of tribute from him.

"It's my last name," she said, holding him with her gaze. "I've got another one, you know."

"I don't need it," he said, trying defiance. "Pendleton will do."

She rose to force him to keep looking into her eyes. "Calling me that makes me sound like a man." She narrowed her eyes. "You do that on purpose, don't you?" she said accusingly. "You're trying to distance yourself from me, aren't you?"

He frowned. "Don't be ridiculous. Why would I want to distance myself from you? You're like my right arm. I couldn't do this job without you. That's the whole point of my being here."

"Yes," she hissed, jabbing her forefinger into his chest. "But you don't want to admit I'm a woman."

"Cut the psychobabble," he said, trying to back away from her but finding himself up against the computer. "It is impossible to forget that you are a woman."

"Then start calling me by my first name. My 'woman' name."

He tried to look scathing but only ended up looking uncomfortable. "Okay, okay. Can we move on?"

"No," she said, still holding him. "Not until you say my name."

His eyes shifted and he rubbed at the place where she'd jabbed him with her finger. "Pendleton, this is ridiculous."

"Say it." She felt a sense of having found the heart of something important. "You're afraid to say it!"

"I am not."

"Then say it."

He licked his lips and tore his gaze away from hers. "Amy," he said quickly. "There. Satisfied?"

"Yes." She smiled at him, eyes glowing. "Oh, yes. You are going to call me Amy from now on. And that's going to change everything."

His brow furled and she could see the P for Pendleton forming on his lips.

"Uh-uh!" she cried, stopped him with another jab at his chest. "It's Amy."

Laughing softly, she spun on her heel and left him standing in the middle of the room.

"This is going to change everything," she whispered to herself as she walked down the hall. And a tiny little part of her heart actually believed it.

Chapter Seven

Amy had planned to make dinner. In fact, she'd bought a couple of steaks and baking potatoes and some fresh broccoli. But as the time for dinner drew near, she got nervous. She'd broiled steaks before. She was pretty sure she could handle it. But messing up tonight would be just too big a failure and she couldn't face it.

Besides, she was very busy all afternoon doing work for Carter, and then she walked the children to the park and watched while they played and by the time they got home, there wasn't much time.

So she ordered a pizza to be delivered.

"What?" Carter said when he got wind of it. "Pizza? Why didn't you tell me? I could have cooked us something good."

"No doubt," she said dryly. "Something simple

like a four-course meal starting off with lobster bisque and ending with crème brûlée. All handmade by you, of course."

"Sounds good to me," he said, but he grinned at her and when she passed his chair, she got the feeling he almost reached out to tousle her hair or something equally friendly.

Almost. Someday, maybe he would feel free enough to go ahead and do it.

She was having a hard time with his reticence. She couldn't figure out why he was so reluctant to make contact. She knew he liked her. In fact, she was pretty sure he liked her a lot. And she thought she'd detected a response from him when that electric connection thing happened between them. So why didn't he follow through?

When she'd first started working for him, he'd had her making arrangements and other reservations for his dates. It hadn't taken long for her to let him know that wasn't what she was hired to do, and he'd very agreeably given the tasks to Delia instead. And Delia had been open about who and when, so Amy hadn't been able to avoid knowing all about it. Carter had still been dating quite a bit in those days, and some of the women had met him at the office before going out. She'd seen them, met them, even had conversations. But she couldn't say she had been jealous of them as they seemed to come and go like yesterday's fashion statements, more ornaments of the moment than real affairs of the heart.

She realized early that he was not in the market for a lasting relationship, no matter how beautiful the lady.

She wondered why. His dating had dropped off lately, and she wondered about that, too. But most of all she wanted to know why he gave her hot looks that could curl her toes, and then tried not to touch her. She was going to ask him, she decided. When the right time came. And her heart started up a rapid beat just thinking about it.

The pizza was pretty good. They all sat around the table, the baby included, and ate the pizza along with a green salad Carter threw together at the last minute. Amy fed the baby creamed spinach with one hand while eating a piece of pizza with the other; feeling like she was beginning to get the hang of such things. The children were acting a little silly, trying to show off for Carter, but this time Amy found herself laughing right along with the rest of them instead of feeling left out. And that was so much better!

Carter went into a long dissertation on the history of pizza, then critiqued the one she'd ordered and mentioned how much better the ones he made were. She laughed at him.

"Carter. With so much domestic experience, how come you've never gotten married?" she asked him lightly when he'd finished his lecture. "I would have thought you would have done it young."

"No. Just the opposite. I don't plan ever to do it at all."

She sat back, suddenly wishing she hadn't brought it up. "That's a little harsh," she murmured.

"You don't understand how badly I wanted to get away from that sort of thing by the time I left it. Just because I knew how, doesn't mean I liked doing it."

He finished off his last piece of pizza and she noted that he'd eaten a lot for someone who thought it was merely mediocre.

"I thought you loved to cook," she noted.

He looked surprised, then a bit chagrined. "I like it pretty well," he admitted. "That's not what I want to avoid. It's more the marriage thing."

That did nothing but annoy her and she couldn't help needling him a little more.

"Oh, that's right. You don't need a wife. You can handle both jobs—husband and wife—with one hand tied behind your back."

He knew she was tweaking him and he wasn't going to give her the satisfaction of getting a rise out of him. "I believe you're right," he said, wiping his mouth with a napkin and staring into her eyes.

She laughed and he smiled and the children began asking what was for dessert. But his answers stuck with her. Why was he so against relationships?

After dinner she bathed the children and put them to bed, one by one, rocking the baby while she read to the two older ones until their eyelids were heavy.

And she called Carter up to kiss them good-night without being asked first.

He came readily, gave them both bear hugs and kisses on their foreheads that made them giggle, then returned to working on the computer. He kept saying he was about to pack things up and head for home, but by nine o'clock, he was still there. She did the dishes, cleaned up the kitchen and finally went into the den to join him.

"Are you going to work all night?" she asked lightly.

"Hmm?" He looked up, then glanced at his watch. "It is getting late. I guess I'll start wrapping things up," he said.

She smiled. She'd heard that one before.

"Oh, you know what?" he said, turning back to her. "Something was in here a while ago, down behind the couch, I think. Making noise. A sort of a scratching sound. I think you've got intruders of some sort. Maybe you ought to call an exterminator."

She nodded sadly but wisely, sinking down into the window seat. "It's Fred," she told him.

His eyebrows knit in a quizzical manner. "Fred? Who's Fred?"

Her eyes got very wide. "Oh, don't you know about Fred? Fred is a little white mouse."

He grunted. "Get a trap."

"Nope. Can't be done. This is a pet mouse."

"Whose pet?"

"Deedee and Scamp's. He got out almost a week ago. We hear him now and then, but we can't catch him."

"If he's that big a pet, you'd think he'd come back on his own."

Amy nodded, looking distressed. "We don't know why Fred would run away. After all, he had all the conveniences of home right there in his little cage."

"Really." It was getting hard for him to rein in a grin. She was playing this little tragedy for all it was worth. He hated to admit how much he liked it when she did this kind of thing. She was just so darn cute.

"Oh, yes," she was saying dramatically. "His own little wheel, his own tiny food dish, fresh water, a fuzzy play toy. What more could a little white mouse want from life?"

"Something you all couldn't give him, obviously." His work on the computer was forgotten. All his attention was on her now and he gave himself up to enjoying her, just for a moment.

"I'm afraid you're right," she said sadly. "Now he's out there somewhere, all alone. Let's just hope some nefarious cat doesn't come strolling through and get a whiff of his scent. I don't think he's had much experience with cats. He might not be on his guard."

That gave him an idea. "Maybe that's why your neighbor's cat is poking around."

"Pooky?" She considered it, frowning thoughtfully. "I don't think so. That cat is too fat to chase anything faster than a snail."

"Hmm. Maybe." He smiled at her, his gaze traveling slowly along her slender arm, skimming quickly over the way her breasts filled out her cotton blouse, lingering along the lines of her beautiful neck. His body was responding and he knew it was time to cut this interlude short.

This was where his iron control usually took over. Usually. But he just couldn't seem to get it in gear tonight. His muscles had a fluid sort of laziness that made his movements slow and there was a strong urge growing in him, an urge to have a woman in his arms. He fought it back with a sense of quick impatience. He wasn't about that sort of thing—especially not with this woman. It really was time to go home.

And yet, he lingered.

"The next time we hear old Fred, I guess I'll have to catch him," he said, watching the way the dim light made shadows along her collarbones, the way her sleek hair framed her pretty face.

"Would you? I would be forever grateful. Believe me, I wasn't looking forward to doing it myself."

There was a silence between them that seemed pregnant with possibilities. She looked at him and then she looked away, suddenly seeming nervous.

"I suppose I ought to go," he said softly, not moving.

She nodded. "It is getting late." She glanced at him, then away again.

"I'll see you tomorrow," he said, still not moving.

She looked at him in surprise. "Tomorrow's Saturday."

"Oh. That's right." He grimaced. "And I'm going to San Francisco on Sunday. Meeting with some executives of Joliet Aire who are stopping over on their way to Japan."

"Ah." Her eyes met his for only a moment and she thought about the fact that, if she still really worked for TriTerraCorp, she would probably be going with him. She couldn't pretend she didn't get a little feeling of regret for just a moment. But that was all she would allow herself.

He shut down his computer and rose from his chair, then stood there, looking down at her.

"You could come along," he said, as though he'd read her mind a few minutes earlier.

She was startled, but shook her head.

"Sure you could," he said, warming to the idea. "We could get a baby-sitter and…"

"Carter, how many times do I have to try to explain this? I'm not going anywhere."

He looked down at the ground and she couldn't read what was going on in his eyes. "Yeah," he said. "Sorry." Then he looked up at her. "You are one loyal sister," he muttered.

She hesitated, then took a deep breath and said,

"Come here," and patted the window seat beside where she was sitting. "Let me tell you about me and my sister. Then maybe you can finally understand."

He came readily enough and dropped down to sit beside her. Their knees touched and the sense of him seemed to fill her head, but she kept her wits about her and began her story.

"Meg and I were close when we were young, even though we seemed to live in separate worlds at times. We were two years apart. And I realize now, looking back, that the focus in our family was always on me. I was the adored younger child, but not only that, I was the one who won the prizes and the scholarships and the awards. I was the ambitious one, the one our parents always went to banquets and awards ceremonies with. Meg was the sweet one and I was the smart one. Meg was the beauty."

He grunted, his blue eyes warm. "You didn't exactly get hit with an ugly stick yourself."

"Well, thank you very much," she said, letting the compliment sink in and smiling. "But when we were young, I paid no attention to that sort of thing at all. I was always looking to excel, while Meg was taking phone calls from boys. I was much too busy for that sort of nonsense." She grinned, remembering. "When we were real little, Meg always played with dolls. I had my own little briefcases."

He laughed, his eyes sparkling. "That's a picture I would like to have seen."

"Right from the beginning I was a go-getter. I wanted to make it to the top, no matter what I was involved in. To be the best. And my parents were so proud of me. It's only been lately, thinking back, that I realize how Meg got shortchanged by it all. She had to give up a lot so that I could succeed. The whole family revolved around me and my various competitions. And poor Meg was always dragged along to witness what a winner I was."

He studied her face. "I still don't see how all this is a bad thing. You had good parents who supported you. You were lucky."

She nodded. "Very true. But it set up a pattern. Even after I became an adult, even after our parents died, I went on expecting Meg to be there for me when I needed her. I expected help with college fees, and I got it, despite the fact that she was struggling herself. What I was doing was always so much more important than anything she might be doing with her life."

She sighed, an ache in her heart for the lost opportunities to appreciate what Meg had always been to her. "She's never called me on it, never complained. It's only been lately that I've begun to realize how unfair all that was to her. And that I need to make amends."

He looked at her quizzically. "So you're taking care of your sister's children to make up for all she did for you over the years."

"If only it were that easy. This is only a small part of the debt I owe her."

He nodded, more to show he was considering what she'd said than to agree with it. He looked at her again. "Don't you see that in some ways, it's a vicious circle?"

She frowned. "What do you mean?"

"I'll lay odds that part of your motivation eventually became to prove to them all that the sacrifices they made were worthwhile. So you had to succeed so that their help would have been worth it. You couldn't let them down. Right?"

She put her head to the side. "Well, there's some truth to that."

"You see, you can't put it all on your own shoulders. It all comes back. I think it's great that you want to make things up to your sister. Very commendable." His eyes seemed to darken as he looked at her. "But don't feel guilty about the past. Gratitude is a very important thing, but guilt will eat away at you like poison. Feel grateful, but don't feel guilty."

His voice was deep and rich with a suppressed emotional intensity that seemed to connect with some emotion she couldn't identify in herself. She could feel it but she wasn't sure what it was. She only knew she vibrated to it like a tuning fork.

"Guilt can destroy your life," he said softly.

She searched his eyes. "You sound like you're talking from experience." Reaching out, she took his hand in hers. ''Carter, what do you feel guilty about?''

For just a moment she thought he was actually going to tell her. He seemed about to. His lips parted and he took a breath, staring down into her eyes, his fingers lacing with hers, his breath on her cheek.

And then he was pulling away, rising, acting as though none of this had happened.

''It really is late,'' he was saying, reaching for his jacket. ''I'd better get going.''

She sat where she was, watching him and wondering if he would ever let go of whatever demon seemed to drive him. He turned back and gave her a fleeting smile.

''Listen, give me a call if you need me tomorrow.''

''I will.''

''Otherwise, I won't see you until Monday.''

She nodded. ''That's right.''

He got all the way to the door before he turned back and said, ''Now don't forget. Call me if you need me.''

''I sure will.''

He stared at her for a long moment, and then he was striding through the house, heading for the front door.

He was in his car very quickly, but he didn't start the engine for a long time. For some reason, he couldn't. He had to decompress. And he realized he was doing exactly what he had sworn he would never do. He had let himself care.

"Hi." Carter stood in the doorway, looking in.

"Hi." Amy stood in front of him, dark eyes shining.

He looked very different from the way she was used to seeing him. Instead of a business suit, he wore faded jeans that fit very snugly and a T-shirt with a logo for a rock group on the front. His muscular biceps were on display and his hair was slightly mussed. She had a fluttery feeling in her chest just looking at him, and a warm temptation toward seduction seeping slowly down through her body. If only she knew what the secret to his tightly controlled libido could be, she would unlock it in a heartbeat.

Still, she couldn't let him know that.

"It's Saturday," she reminded him. "We don't work on Saturday. Why are you here?"

He looked thoughtful, frowning. "That's not true. We often work on Saturday."

She shook her head firmly. "Only when there's a deadline or a big project or a trip or something like that."

His wide mouth twisted in a slow grin. "Which is just about all the time."

She made a face, admitting it. "True."

Their gazes tangled for a moment and Amy felt breathless by the time they both looked away.

"Anyway, I thought I ought to stop by," he said, shifting his weight. "You never called."

She gave him a look of surprise. "It's not even noon yet."

"I know." He frowned again, refusing to give even a hint of embarrassment. "But I thought you might have tried to call when I was in the shower. Or something."

"No." Her smile curled her lips and felt warm even to her. "I didn't call you."

"Oh." He gazed at her levelly, daring her to tell him to go away.

She bit her lip and then gave in to the temptation to tease him a little. "You said to call if I needed you. And…" She shrugged elaborately and said it proudly, to prove she was handling things. "I didn't need you."

Something flared in his eyes. She watched, fascinated, as he brought the emotion, whatever it was, under control again.

"You didn't need me," he echoed, that emotion just barely in check. "Well, hell, Pendleton. Maybe I needed you."

Her shock at that statement was so great, she could only murmur, "It's Amy, not Pendleton." He was already in the house and moving toward the kitchen and acting as though nothing unusual had happened. Or been said. She followed him, feeling just a little dazed.

"Anyway, I thought I ought to come by and see

if I could catch that mouse for you," he said as he went, glancing at her sideways. "Wouldn't want to leave that until Monday."

"Oh. Of course."

"And I stopped and picked up some doughnuts." He held up the box.

"Oh, how nice." She laughed. She was feeling very happy all of a sudden. Happy, but a bit confused. "We are awash in great food lately. Paul brought over some blueberry muffins he baked this morning."

Carter stared at her, almost rolling his eyes, then said through gritted teeth, "Muffins, huh? Let's see them."

She led him on into the kitchen and pointed out the pretty little muffins arranged on a plate and covered with plastic wrap.

He scoffed. "You call those muffins?" Discarding the box of doughnuts in the corner as though they no longer mattered, he began to roll up his sleeves. "I'll show you muffins. Where are your muffin tins?"

She gaped at him. She couldn't believe it. He was going to take Paul's gift as another challenge. "Carter…"

"Got any blueberries?"

She shook her head, barely controlling her laughter.

"How about dried cranberries? They'll do."

She went to a drawer where she knew Meg kept

such things and pulled out a bag bursting with the little crimson delights.

"Great," he said, turning on the oven, moving around the kitchen with cool efficiency. "Did you show him the cookies I made?"

"No, of course not." She gazed at him in astonishment. "What did you want to do, rub his nose in it? Do you want him to admit you beat him at cookie-making?"

"Damn right I do." He opened the refrigerator, hunting for eggs. "And I'm going to beat him at muffins, too. You wait and see."

She sighed, shaking her head. "Men," she muttered.

"What was that?"

"Oh, nothing."

Laughing softly, she left him to his baking. She had children to take care of.

But the moment she was alone, the memory of him saying, "Maybe I needed you," came back and she caught her breath in her throat and put her hand over her heart. Had he really said it? Was she dreaming?

She took the children into the front yard to play, letting the baby reach for butterflies while Deedee tried out a mini-Big Wheel toy and Scamp chased imaginary demons through the bushes. All in all, she was already feeling more comfortable with them. It got better every day. They were good kids and she only had to admonish Scamp about twenty times not to climb on the porch railing, which looked rickety and could land him on the rock garden below if he were to slip. Unfortunately, the railings had been structured to look almost like a jungle gym and seemed to tempt the little boy as nothing else did.

An hour later she brought them back into the house, set them down with puzzles and books and went back to the kitchen, ready to begin fixing lunch. Carter was wrapping up his bakery project.

"So you're done," she said, looking around him to see the finished product where it sat on the counter.

He'd done it again. His muffins were golden-brown, huge and light as a feather. Paul's looked like the "before" picture sitting next to them.

"You are an exceptionally good cook," she admitted when she tasted one.

"Of course I am," he said, as though it were only natural. "I'm good at everything I do."

He turned and looked into her eyes as he said it, as though he meant to convey a message and didn't want her to miss it. Her heart caught, skipped a beat, and began to race. She had to turn away to avoid embarrassing herself, muttering something about hearing a child call so that she could escape.

But she didn't go looking for the children. She just needed to get out of his presence for a moment, to quiet her breathing and to settle her heart. This was getting ridiculous. It was so bad, all he had to do was catch her gaze and she was sailing on a sensual wind that might take her just about anywhere. She had to get better control.

"Either that," she whispered to herself, "or lose control altogether."

And her heart began to pound again at the very thought of losing control with Carter.

She gave the children muffins and soup for lunch, while Carter spent the time hunting for Fred.

"Just show me the last place you heard him and I'll give it a try," he said, grabbing a flashlight and a paper bag.

"Fred was in my room this mornin'," Scamp told Carter very seriously. "Don' hurt him."

"I won't hurt him," Carter promised.

But Deedee and Scamp both seemed apprehensive as they ate their lunch and had to run to see what Carter was doing as soon as they were excused. Amy cleared the table and washed the dishes before following them. Carter had the children's room torn apart, but no sighting of the little mouse had been made. At least, not by Carter.

"I thought I heard him once," Carter said, scratching his head. "I took every single thing out of the closet, but we didn't see him."

"I saw him!" Scamp cried, jumping up and down. "I did!"

"Me, too," Deedee chimed in, trying to jump but not making it off the floor.

Carter frowned. "Scamp says he saw him. But I

sure didn't.'' He looked at Amy. "Say, do you have a picture of Fred?''

Amy blinked. "A picture? Carter, he's a white mouse.''

"Well, I can't see him," he repeated, frustrated and dragging his fingers through his hair. "And I know he's there. At least, I thought he was for a while. So I thought, maybe I'm looking for the wrong visual clues. If I just had a picture…''

She swore she wouldn't laugh, but it was getting harder to avoid it. "Carter, you know what a white mouse looks like? Picture it in your mind.'' She put a hand on his arm and leaned closer, saying earnestly, "Fred looks just like that.''

He didn't seem to find it a joking matter. "Have you ever seen him?'' he demanded.

"No. He got out the day I came, before I had a chance to be introduced.''

"Then how do you know?''

She hesitated. He had a point. "Scamp, do you have a picture of Fred?''

Scamp shook his head of white-gold hair. "Maybe he's a ghost mouse,'' he suggested helpfully, his eyes huge.

"There you go,'' Carter said, nodding as though the point were the most valid he'd heard all day. "I can't see him because he's invisible.''

Amy sighed. "That's going to make it that much harder to catch him, isn't it?''

Carter grinned. "Not for us.'' He jerked his head

at the children. "Come on, gang. On to the living room."

Picking up his flashlight and paper bag, he led the procession, the younger ones marching behind him and giggling. Amy watched them go, her hands on her hips and a smile on her lips. It was actually a joy to watch him with the children. But then, more and more she was beginning to realize she could watch him do almost anything and get a charge out of it.

"Watch out, girl," she told herself as she began putting back all the things they had pulled out in their search. "If you're not careful, you're going to find yourself falling in love."

Chapter Eight

"You'd better take the children out of here." Carter looked at Amy sternly, then glanced back to where Deedee and Scamp were looking under the bed. He lowered his voice to make sure they wouldn't hear. "In fact, why don't you go ahead and put them down for naps?"

"What do you mean?" Amy was game, but not sure why he wanted this done.

He leaned closer and said in a low voice, "I'm going to catch this little rodent and I can't guarantee it's going to be pretty." He gave her a significant look. "If there were to be an accident, I wouldn't want them to know about it."

She gasped softly, shifting the baby from one hip to the other. "Oh, I see what you mean."

She did as he suggested, starting with the baby,

who was half asleep in her arms anyway, and then the two older kids. And all the time she was thinking that despite everything and against her better judgment, it was just so darn much fun having Carter around.

She'd always liked him. And they had always worked together like a well-oiled machine. But now she realized that one of the foundations to their relationship was just how much they enjoyed being together. If only she could think of a way to make their time with each other last for years and years... Oh, well, that didn't seem to be in the cards. But a part of her yearned for him in a strange, inexplicable way, considering he was in the house with her. But she knew she wasn't really satisfied with the side of him she got to see. She wanted more. Much, much more.

When she came down from the children's room, she found Carter coming in the front door, looking rather pleased with himself.

"Where have you been?" she asked him.

He gave her a look that was meant to be innocent, but ended up being anything but. "I took some of my cookies and muffins over to Paul," he said blithely. "To thank him for the ones he brought over here."

Her jaw dropped. "Oh, to thank him! Right." She shook her head, astonished. "I can't believe you did that."

He shrugged. "It was a neighborly fair

exchange,'' he stated. ''I'm a neighborly kind of guy.''

''It was a blatant attempt to show him yours were better,'' she countered.

He looked at her for a moment, then gave up all pretenses. ''Well, of course it was. What is the point of beating him out when he doesn't know he's been beat? I had to show him.''

She groaned, half laughing, feeling only sympathy for what Paul must be going through at that moment. He was too nice a man for this. What had he ever done to deserve having Carter on his trail?

''Anyway, are the kids down?'' he asked, dismissing the whole thing as old news. ''I'd better get back to work on this mouse situation.''

''The kids are down,'' she told him, still snickering. ''And I'm ready to assist you in any way I can,'' she added with a smart salute.

''Good.''

''Only...be careful, won't you? Poor little Fred. He's really become quite a favorite of mine.''

He gave her a baleful look. ''You've never seen him face-to-face.''

''No,'' she said serenely. ''But I can feel his presence. In the spiritual sense.''

'' 'In the spiritual sense,' '' he repeated, mocking her. ''Great. Next thing we know you'll be channeling Mickey Mouse.'' He handed her the flashlight along with a look that told her he thought she was pretty darn cute, despite his words. "Okay. Let's get to work."

Meg and Tim's bedroom was down the hall from where the children were sleeping, far enough away so that they wouldn't have to be afraid of being heard by the little ones as they went on their mouse hunt. Amy slept in it every night, but she looked at it with fresh eyes as they entered. It was a very nice room with a king-size bed, a bureau and a dresser, a full-length mirror and a large bookcase along one wall. The bay window looked out over the backyard and right into the branches of an old oak tree.

"Where was he when you heard him last?" Carter whispered to her, gazing around at every nook and cranny.

She suppressed a smile and tried to stay serious. "Under the bed. And in the closet, actually. In fact…"

Her voice trailed off and her eyes widened. "Listen," she whispered, motioning him toward the closet.

They both listened. There was no doubt about it. A small furtive sound was coming from one of the upper shelves.

Their gazes met and Carter grinned.

"Got him!" he mouthed to her. "Here, hold this," he whispered, handing her the flashlight. "Hand it to me when I tell you to."

"But…"

"Shh!"

He pulled a handy little stepladder over to use to reach the top shelf. Amy looked at it uneasily. It seemed a bit rickety and Carter was a big guy. But he climbed up and it seemed to be holding.

"Okay," he whispered, reaching out a hand while his gaze was fixed on the space between boxes on the shelf. "Hand me the flashlight."

She reached up to hand it to him and he reached down to take it. At the same time, there was a cracking sound, and suddenly the step had given way and he was plunging through the air toward her.

"Watch out!" he cried.

"Oh!"

The next thing they knew, they were both sprawled on the floor, Amy situated beneath Carter, in an awkward, convoluted way. Looking up, she found his face just above hers. He was looking down into her eyes. They both started laughing at the same time.

"Are you okay?" he asked her.

"I think so. How about you?"

"Nothing hurts at the moment," he said. But he made no attempt to move.

"Uh… We seem to be tangled together." She was only mentioning it in case he hadn't noticed.

"Yes, we do."

Was it her imagination or did his voice seem lower, sort of sultry and interesting?

"I wonder how this happened," she murmured.

"It was Fred's fault," he said even more softly. "Darn mouse."

His body felt so right against hers. She heard a heart beating and wasn't sure if it was hers or his. Or maybe, both.

"Carter," she said softly, feeling brave. "Have you ever wanted to kiss me?"

He didn't hesitate. "Many times," he admitted, his voice a low rumble.

She sighed. "Well, here's your chance. This seems like an awfully good time for you to do it."

She half expected his expression to harden and for him to jump up and start pretending they'd never been plastered together against the floor. But this time, he didn't do that. For once, he followed through on what his eyes were telling her he really wanted to do.

She closed her eyes and he kissed her, gently at first, barely a touch, but enough to send a thrill down her bloodstream.

And that was supposed to be all. Now they'd kissed and it was time for her to open her eyes and for him to pull back and laugh in an unconcerned manner, and for them to get up off the floor and go on with things. After all, this was their very first kiss. It should be short and sweet, just a token of affection, maybe a bit of an exploration, but basically innocent. She knew very quickly that wasn't the way it was going to be.

The kiss took on a life of its own and suddenly

she was accepting his mouth, parting her lips and inviting his tongue inside, gasping as it slid provocatively deeper. He was all heat and strength moving against her and she felt herself respond with a deep, rich hunger that made her moan low in her throat and arch beneath him, relishing the feel of him.

She wanted to open her legs, too, she wanted to feel him rub against her, she wanted his tongue on her breasts...

"Oh!" she cried, her eyes snapping open and her hands balling into fists against his chest. "Stop!"

He pulled back reluctantly and she could tell he was short of breath, just as she was. She stared at him in confusion. She'd kissed men before. She knew what she was doing. But she hadn't been prepared to find her own body and soul turn traitor with such enthusiasm. That had never happened to her before.

"Wow," she said. "You ought to wear a Danger—High Explosives sign, or something."

He laughed, dropping a quick kiss on her lips and vaulting to his feet before holding out a hand to help her up.

"Amy," he said, and then stopped, looking at her luminously.

Her heart stuttered and almost stopped. This was the first time he'd used her name without prompting. Just the sound of it on his lips made it new. She bit her lip, as much to keep herself from blurting that she loved him as anything else. She knew, despite what had just happened, that he didn't want to hear that. She wasn't sure she wanted to hear it herself.

"Amy, I didn't mean for that to happen."

"I know you didn't," she said calmly.

His kiss had ignited a fire that was going to smolder in her no matter what he did in the future. Still, she felt oddly satisfied for now. He'd finally acknowledged the pull that existed between them. That was something she'd thought at times he never would do.

"You may not have meant for it to happen," she said. "But I did." She gave him an impish grin and backed out of the room, leaving him behind as she went downstairs, ostensibly to see about some cleaning she knew needed to be done.

Once out of his sight, her bravado faded and she slipped into the bathroom, locked the door and leaned on the sink with both hands, her eyes closed, her soul reeling. She could still feel his lips on hers, still remember the sound of his heartbeat, still feel the excitement of his body heat against hers.

What would it be like to be his lover? Right now she couldn't imagine anything more wonderful. Her body seemed to quiver as she formed the thought. But she wasn't going to kid herself. She knew it was futile to try to dream of building a future with him. There was nothing but the moment. Was that enough?

To live in the moment—that was stupid and she knew it. Ridiculous, self-defeating, the way women had run into trouble throughout the ages, and here she was ready to consider it. You had to pay for that kind of thinking—pay big time. Could she afford it?

"No," she told herself fiercely. "You know better. You're too smart and too secure in yourself to let that happen."

And yet, something deep inside yearned for him with an intensity that burned so strongly she could hardly stand it, and it took some time before she felt calm enough to leave the cool and reasonable protection of the bathroom.

When he left, about an hour later, he still hadn't caught Fred. But there was a new sense of intimacy between them, and that couldn't be denied. The look in Carter's eyes whenever his gaze fell on her told her he wasn't going to be able to pretend nothing was happening here any longer, and that he had pretty much admitted that to himself. That he felt that way filled her with joy. That there still was no real future for them filled her with despair.

"So, basically," she concluded as she watched him drive off into the late afternoon, "you're walking around with a split personality for the time being."

That about summed it up. Still, it was better than a toothache.

Carter stared out the window of the commuter plane on the flight from San Francisco, watching the little square houses get bigger and bigger as the

plane descended. He was back along the central
coast, just an hour from Rio de Oro and Amy.

No, not Amy. He'd promised himself he wasn't
going to go by the house or call Amy—or even think
about her today.

Of course, the last had been impossible to comply
with. He'd spent most of his time all day thinking
about her and how she wasn't there with him as she
should be. Everywhere he went, she seemed to trail
him in the air, like a scent that made you remember
a day out of your past. He kept thinking how she
would have enjoyed this trip to San Francisco with
him—how she would have laughed at various inci-
dents, such as when the dog entangled his owner in
a leash on Market Street, how she would have loved
the raw oysters at the Top of the Mark bar, how she
would have spoken to the Joliet Aire executives in
French and made things much more pleasant than
they had been without her.

Not that things had gone badly. No, the executives seemed predisposed to using TriTerraCorp for
the resort development project. Only Monsieur
Jobert, who was still in Paris, was still undecided,
and everything rode on his approval. And best of
all, Jobert had agreed to call them Monday night.
So it was coming down to the wire. If he and Amy
landed this contract, they would both be the fair-
haired children at TriTerraCorp. They would pretty
much be able to write their own ticket just about
anywhere in the real-estate development world.

Would Amy come back to work if that happened? Of course she would. She would see how much she got out of it and she wouldn't be able to turn him down. She had done a good job taking over the child care for her sister and he admired her for doing it. But enough was enough. For all the compassion he had for her, he had to smile. He could see that she didn't really care for the domestic routine. She wasn't used to it, but she also had no affinity for it. After all, she'd been a go-getter from the get-go. From what she'd told him, even as a child she'd preferred winning ribbons to playing house. She was born with certain talents and who could blame her for wanting to use them to the full extent of her abilities?

No, she hadn't found the same sense of accomplishment with the kids. And that pretty much assured that she would be coming back to work with him. After a few weeks in this hell, she would be begging for her old job back.

And that was certainly a relief. He hadn't known what he would do without her and now he was pretty sure he wasn't going to have to learn. As for this new sexual tension that buzzed between them— well, there was one very good way to take care of that. And it didn't require a wedding ring.

He exited the plane and headed for the walkway, trying to remember where he'd parked his car. He was going to go home and take a shower and relax, maybe find a ballgame on the television. And he wasn't going to worry about Amy and the kids.

It had only been about twenty-four hours since he'd seen them. What could happen in that short a time, anyway?

The only possibility was if maybe Fred had been sighted. Or Paul had come over with more of his inedible offerings. Or maybe one of the kids had gotten sick. What if something like that had happened? She was there all alone. It would be tough trying to take care of a sick or injured kid with the other two hanging on her. Even seasoned veterans of child care would be hard pressed to make a success of a situation like that.

Maybe he'd better just give her a quick call, just to make sure everything was okay. Turning, he scanned the long walkway, looking for a likely place to use his cell phone, and at the same time he'd already flipped it open and started punching in her number.

Amy sat back in the garden chair and closed her eyes and just relaxed, enjoying the feel of the sun on her face. It was amazing how just having another adult around changed things. The level of tension was way down. When things went wrong, Amy knew there was hope—that she wasn't staring down into an abyss of helplessness. And knowing that made it that much easier to deal with the little ups and downs the children had on any normal day.

She still felt as though a tornado had scooped her up a week or so ago and hadn't set her back down yet. But at least she could see solid land beneath her now and had some hope of a soft landing. Without Carter's help, she might have let the whirlwind beat her to a sorry pulp.

But that wasn't happening, and in fact, she was getting better and better at dealing with children, and at the same time, she was getting an hour or so of time to fold in business work, as well. Not bad.

Tonight Carter would be staying very late, as they were expecting the telephone call from Monsieur Jobert. If they could actually finagle a contract out of all this while she wasn't even officially working for the company, that would be quite a coup for them—for the partnership that they formed together.

Ah, togetherness. She rather liked it.

Carter was in the den right now, working on contracts, and she would go in anytime now to help him. But for the moment, she wanted to savor her happiness. All in all, things were going pretty well.

"Aun' Amy! Deedee says she got to go potty."

"Okay, Scamp. I'm coming."

Well, so much for her little interlude. She was rapidly learning that mothers didn't get much time for savoring things. They had to catch their joy on the fly. But that only made it that much sweeter— or so she'd been told. She wasn't really sure if she bought that one yet. Rising with only marginal regret, she headed back into the house.

* * *

"You know what? I'm actually nervous."

Amy was sitting cross-legged on the couch and Carter was working on the computer, but what they were both doing was waiting for the call from France.

"Nervous is good," he said, barely glancing up from the screen. "It gives you an adrenaline rush and makes you do better."

"Right," she said. "Until it makes you do worse."

"You won't do worse." He gave up on the computer work and rose, dropping down to sit beside her on the couch. They both stared at the telephone.

"I hate waiting," she fretted, waving a hand in the air. "Call already!"

He frowned at her. "Hey, this isn't like you. You're usually so calm and in control."

"I've changed," she retorted, turning to laugh into his face. "It's been a life-changing week for me. Hadn't you noticed?"

"It has, hasn't it?" He grinned at her. "But you've done fine. And remember, this will only last another few weeks. Then you'll be free again."

She nodded, feeling speculative. "It is quite an experience," she said. "I have learned a lot. And not just about changing diapers. Also about myself and what I want out of life."

Carter waited expectantly. This was exactly what

he wanted to hear. But she didn't go on in the direction he'd hoped for.

Frowning thoughtfully, she looked to him for an answer. "But here's what I don't understand." She spread her hands, palms up. "After barely surviving this week, I really wonder. How do single mothers do it? Without another adult to help, I would think they would be jumping out of windows all over town."

He looked at her oddly, his eyes hooded. "It's very tough. There are some real heroines out there who sacrifice their own happiness to raise their children on their own. And then again, there are some who don't make it."

Amy shook her head. "Poor things," she said softly, looking worried.

He watched the expressions change on her face and decided she only got more beautiful every time he looked at her. He loved seeing her with her hair in a tangled cloud around her face, with her hair hanging down around her shoulders, or as it was now, pulled back in a professional-style twist. Any way she did it, she looked great.

But she still seemed to be waiting for him to tell her something about single mothers for some reason. He cast about for something new to say.

"One of the best ideas I've heard of is where a bunch of single mothers get together in a co-op and rent a house. It works out best if they each have jobs at different times of the day. Then they can take turns with the cooking, cleaning, child care, and everything else.''

"How about putting a single father in there, too?" Amy suggested. "Then the kids have a male role model."

"Oh, no," he said, suddenly laughing. "You introduce a male into the mix and you've got trouble."

"Trouble?"

He nodded, eyes dancing. "Romance is bound to rear its ugly head."

Her mouth dropped in outrage. He was always so negative about relationships. "Why do you call romance 'ugly'?"

His eyes widened innocently. "Did I?"

"Yes. You did."

"It was just a figure of speech. I don't think you need to assign psychological motives to it."

"Don't you?" She glared at him. "I don't know, Carter James. Something tells me you have a very slanted outlook on life. What happened to your childhood to screw you up like this?" She was only half joking and as the words came out, she wished she could call them back when she saw the change in his eyes.

He was quiet for a moment, then said softly, "My mother was a single mom, you know."

He grimaced and half took it back. "Well, not a single mom exactly. I guess that implies never having been married. She was more a deserted mom who ended up having to do it on her own."

Amy remembered he'd said something about this before, but she'd forgotten all about it. "How many children did you say were in the family?"

"Six. I was the oldest."

"Six!" Amy's mind reeled at the concept. Now that she'd had this experience, she could understand just what that meant. "How did she manage?"

"She didn't. Not really. We were a mess. And she died much too young."

Amy sat back and watched him with huge dark eyes, her hands folded in her lap. "Tell me," she said simply.

He looked at her. He wasn't going to do that. He didn't tell people about his background. Never had, never would. It was nobody's business and he started to tell her so.

But for some reason, he found himself telling her the whole story instead—a story he himself hadn't thought about for many years, a story he definitely had never told anyone else. He hadn't even let himself think about it. It wasn't a very comforting or pleasant story, and it wasn't anything he was particularly proud of. But for the first time in his life, the story poured out of him, and once he got started, he couldn't seem to stop the flow.

He told her quickly how his father left the family when he was young, leaving him to do a lot of the parenting to the little ones as his mother was often ill. Though that left him little time to do what young boys usually did as they grew up, he felt very responsible at an early age and worked hard for his family.

"My mother got really sick when I was about fourteen. From then on it was a constant round of hospitals, then back home nursing her, and then back to the hospital again."

"What did she have?"

"Some kind of cancer. I don't even remember all the details clearly now. I pretty much blocked it out as much as I could."

When he was fifteen, his mother died.

"Just before she let go, she made me promise to keep the family together. We didn't have any relatives to help out and she was frantic, worrying about the younger ones. So I promised her."

For more than a year he managed to hold off social services with lies, telling them his father was back, telling them anything he could think of to keep them from breaking up the family. But eventually the truth came out and the children were split up to go to foster homes—a move that had devastated him almost as much as losing his mother had.

"I hated that, having the younger ones go to strangers. It killed me. I felt like I'd let my mother down to let it happen."

"Carter, you were just a kid. That was much too much responsibility for a boy that age to carry on his shoulders."

He shrugged, his blue eyes dark with a haunting

regret. "It was my job to see that the family stayed together. I blew it."

Running away from his own foster home, he'd lied about his age and joined the army, getting a college education in the process and earning a grant that put him through a good graduate business school.

And he worked very hard to do well at it, his driving goal to gather his family together again once he had enough money to take care of them all. When he finally felt he'd made that, he went looking for his brothers and sisters.

The first one he found was Callie, the sister who was closest to him in age. He went to see her, filled with anticipation. And it was wonderful to see her again. But she was entrenched in a new life and didn't really need him or want him to do anything to change her circumstances. And the others were the same, each involved in a new family, each with his own life to live. The youngest barely knew who he was.

Watching as he told her about all this, Amy could see that it broke his heart. Everything he'd lived for over the years seemed to crumble into dust for him at that time. As he said, he'd blown it. Now she understood where he'd learned about guilt and how to get over it before it ate away at your life. The only question she had was whether he'd really gotten over it at all. But when she tried to bring it up, he scoffed at her theory.

"I moved on, Pendleton," he said, and she winced as he reverted to his old habit. "All that just fell into the pattern of my life. I mean, I lost my father, my mother, and then all my siblings. No big surprise." He realized he sounded bitter and he softened it with a smile as she took up his hand and held it in her own, her sympathy clear in her dark eyes.

"Hey, I figured out long ago that all I was going to care about was business. At least there you get back what you put into things. Human relationships just don't pay off."

"Oh, Carter!" She squeezed his hand and brought it up to her cheek. "Don't say things like that."

"Why not? It's true."

She shook her head, denying it. "Do you ever see any of your brothers or sisters now?" she asked him.

"No," he said shortly. "We have nothing in common. There's no reason to see each other."

But she saw the pain in his eyes and she ached to do something to heal him. "Carter—" she began, leaning close.

The telephone rang and they both jumped into the air, startled.

"Oh!" Amy cried. She'd forgotten all about the call from France. "Here it is! Now if I can just keep from forgetting all the French I ever learned…"

Chapter Nine

Amy hung up the phone almost a half hour later and turned slowly to face Carter, staring at him as though she'd been shell-shocked. "He's coming," she whispered.

"What?"

He'd been waiting, trying to filter out a French word here and there, trying to judge how things were going by her tone, but finally giving up. Right now he hadn't a clue how things had gone.

She took in a deep breath, eyes shining with excitement. "He's coming!" she cried.

"He's coming? He's coming here?"

She nodded.

"Whoa!" Carter grabbed her hands and pulled her to her feet and they began to dance around the floor. "He's coming! He's coming!"

She threw her arms around his neck and then he was kissing her firmly on the lips and the dancing came to a stop. Just as suddenly as they had exploded with joy, they were now caught up in the passion that had been simmering between them for as long as they had known each other.

The room fell away. Reality fell away. Good sense fell away, and Amy was spinning in a sensual fog that took her breath away. His mouth was hot on hers, his tongue a rasping provocateur that seemed to arouse her as she'd never been aroused before. They fell together onto the couch, kissing deeply, clinging together.

"Amy," he whispered huskily, his arms winding around her and holding her tightly. "Oh, Amy…"

She sighed happily, doubts pushed aside. All she wanted in the world was to revel in the feel of him against her. The ecstasy of it was almost more than she could bear. She ran her hands up his hard chest and kneaded her fingers into his muscles and stretched like a cat.

He pulled away her sweater and dug into her lacy bra to bring her breast into view. She arched to his touch, moaning as he played with the tight, hard nipple. She began to ache for him. Her need grew quickly and became so urgent, her hips moved with it of their own accord. She wanted him and she wanted him now. Her mind blurred with desire and she wimpered, reaching for him and wondering why he wasn't pulling off his belt and coming to her.

"Amy."

He'd said her name but she didn't respond.

"Amy!"

She realized blearily that he'd stopped touching her. Raising her head, she looked at his face.

"What?" she asked him impatiently.

"Amy..." He wrapped his arms around her and held her close. "Amy, I want to make love to you. I want it more than anything. But I don't think this is a good time."

"Why not?"

"Because I think it's a decision you should make with a clear head. We're going too fast. We ought to hold back a little. Make sure."

She took a shuddering breath and closed her eyes, her head cradled against his chest. He was right and she knew it. As her good sense came back, she sighed. He was absolutely right, and such a good guy, she could hardly stand it. Tears came and she blinked them back. Could she tell him how much she loved him now? Or should that wait, too?

"We need to start planning," he reminded her softly, still holding her as gently as a baby. "Monsieur Jobert is a formidable negotiator."

She raised her head, her eyes suddenly bright. "Ohmigod," she said, jumping back. "He's going to be here in two weeks. What are we going to do?"

Two weeks seemed like plenty of time, but there was a lot to do in getting ready to give the best presentation they were capable of, and they both worked very hard on it. Carter moved his personal items into the den, sleeping on the couch and working on the computer long into the night. Meanwhile, Amy gave him every minute she could wrench away from the children.

"But the kids come first," she reminded him time and time again.

"I know, I know," he retorted impatiently. "But I come somewhere along the line. I need you, too."

It was lovely to be needed, she had to admit. But sometimes it was a bit draining, especially when everyone in the house needed you at the same time.

She'd begun taking Scamp to preschool three days a week—a practice that had been suspended the first week after the accident—and that gave her more time to concentrate on Deedee. She liked doing simple things with her, like taking her into the backyard to watch snails head for cover on sunny mornings or feeding the fish in the fishpond or trying to teach her to sing "Monkeys on the Bed."

"How many is four?" she would ask. Deedee would hold up four fingers, watching her aunt's face apprehensively, and Amy would cry, "Yes!" and give her a hug and Deedee would laugh uproariously.

Amy was finding that there was joy in children, and not just drudgery.

She found time every afternoon to run to the hospital to visit with Meg and sometimes with Tim, as well. It was amazing how quickly they were healing. Meg looked stronger every time she saw her and she was so anxious to get back to her children, she could hardly contain herself.

"My babies will have grown so much I'll hardly recognize them," she fretted. "I hate that I'm missing out on a chunk of their life like this. I'm supposed to be there."

"You will be," Amy told her, giving her a quick kiss on the forehead. "They miss you like crazy, but they will still be there when you get home, arms open wide."

"Thanks to you." Meg's eyes filled with tears. "Oh, Amy, I can't tell you how much I appreciate all you've done. How will I ever make it up to you?"

"Don't you dare even talk like that," Amy insisted. "This is payback for all you've done for me over the years. I can't even begin to even the score."

But at least she had begun the process. When she had time to think about it, she was glad she'd taken things in hand and done this for Meg. It had made a big difference in her life and in her outlook. She knew more about herself and more about the world than she ever had in her previously tunnel-visioned life. In some ways it had set her free.

She was easier and less uptight with the children now. She could tell they responded better to her than they had before. She was just as likely to help Carter in the den with baby Jillian on her hip as she worked as she was to put the baby down first, and Jillian seemed to thrive with all the holding she was getting. With the other two, she was easy and affectionate and not quite as concerned with rules and regulations as she had been at first. Deedee sometimes spontaneously crawled up into her lap now, and Scamp brought her bugs and rocks he wanted to identify.

But the work rumbled on beneath it all. They were frantically racing to ready a killer presentation. Getting the contract with Joliet Aire meant convincing Monsieur Jobert that they could deliver on the best the development world had to offer. If they succeeded, they would be heroes at TriTerraCorp. If they failed—well, life would go on, but some of the luster would fade away.

"We've got to get this contract," Carter would say at least ten times a day, usually through gritted teeth.

But Carter also had other things on his mind. And the rivalry with the next-door neighbor was at the top of his list. Something about the man just seemed to rub him the wrong way.

Toward the middle of the second week, Paul brought over a quiche Lorraine he had made, and even Carter had to admit it was to die for.

"He's outdone himself on this one," he allowed, sampling a large bite. He frowned. "I wonder if he had to call in help."

"Oh, Carter." Amy cut herself a nice big slice. It was delicious.

Carter finished his piece, then watched her eat hers, noting how she savored every bite. "Well, there's nothing else for it," he said at last. "Invite him over for dinner."

Amy's eyebrows rose. "Are you ready to make friends?" she asked hopefully.

"Friends? What are you talking about? I'm ready to make a gourmet meal that will knock his socks off."

She put down her fork and glared at him. "I can't believe this. What is your problem?"

"I don't have the problem. Your friend Paul is the one with the problem. He's got to try to beat me at cooking and he can't do it."

Her shoulders sagged. This was so ridiculous, she kept thinking he must be joking. But he looked absolutely serious, and that worried her. How far would these men go with this strange rivalry?

She took a deep breath and let it out, still glaring at him. Finally she leaned forward and said icily, "There's nothing more embarrassing than watching two grown men in a 'mine is bigger than yours' contest."

He looked surprised that she would say such a thing. "That's not what this is. I wouldn't be so immature." His face was the picture of guilelessness. "This is all about 'mine is *better* than yours'."

"Oh." She waved her hand in the air. "You're

right. That is so much more mature. What was I thinking?''

Reluctantly, she invited Paul over and he came with what looked to her like some trepidation. But Carter was perfectly pleasant to him, offering him a before-dinner drink and then treating them all to a dinner that was out of this world. He did it all without any help, producing beautifully presented platters of grilled prosciutto-wrapped prawns smothered in garlic butter, asparagus tips in lemon hollandaise sauce, a couscous and wild mushroom pilaf with a bruschetta appetizer and an arugula and grapefruit salad. It was heavenly.

They had quite a nice time and Paul was generous with his praise. Carter was charming as he could be and his feathers seemed to have been smoothed down for the time being.

When Carter left them in the living room together while he went into the kitchen to fix dessert, Paul smiled at Amy and paid her a nice compliment. That made her think she ought to make sure he understood where things stood.

"Paul, you're such a nice guy. It's just…well, I feel like I have to tell you…"

"That you're in love with your boss," he said with a wicked smile.

She blinked. "Is it really that obvious?"

"Yes." He laughed. "And I must admit I'm sorry that things turned out that way. It galls me to know he's the best cook, and he also gets the best prize."

"The best prize?"

"You, Amy. You're a gift from God for any man who wins you. My hat's off to him."

Amy glowed. Praise like that was hard to come by and she didn't want to let it go too easily. She only wished that Carter had heard it.

But then again, maybe it was just as well he hadn't. She wouldn't have wanted to revive the competition between the two men. And anyway, it was getting more and more of a chore to keep Carter at bay.

They had not had a repeat of the passionate encounter on the couch the night of the telephone call from France. Amy was so glad Carter had found the good sense that night to stop what began to happen. Now that she'd had time to think it over, she knew an affair was not in her own best interests, nor was it in Carter's. He'd been right to tell her to go slow.

The only trouble was, he seemed to have forgotten his own good advice now. He was making a habit of cornering her at any chance moment and snatching hungry kisses that quickly turned torrid. It was difficult to keep fending him off, especially since she wanted him as much as he wanted her. Maybe more. She'd admitted how she felt for longer.

"We can't keep doing this," she'd panted after one passionate interlude in the kitchen after the children had gone to bed.

"Why not?" he murmured, snacking on her neck.

RAYE MORGAN   159

"You know very well why." She pushed him back. "This is transitional stuff. It leads to other things."

His hands slid down her sides and captured her bottom, pulling it into the hard hunger of his hips. "It doesn't have to," he lied as he reveled in the feel of her.

"Yes, it does," she insisted, pulling away, breathless and quivering. "That's the nature of the beast, so to speak." She backed away from him with regret, but determination. There was just no way she was going to start an affair with her boss in her sister's house, with her nieces and nephew sleeping a few feet away. Not while she had her head about her, at any rate.

And he understood that. He didn't really press her. But every time their eyes met, she felt how hot the fire was between them, and she knew she was going to have to make a firm decision very soon.

In the meantime, life was deliciously exciting with Carter in the house. And the children were a hoot, as well.

It was Scamp who finally caught Fred.

The morning had started out slow and sleepy and Carter and Amy were talking softly over morning coffee when he came running down the hallway, still in his Star Wars pajamas.

"Aun' Amy! Come quick! I found Fred."

They dropped everything and followed him to the laundry room. There was the little mouse snuggled down in an old shirt that had been left in the corner, surrounded by little pink bundles of joy.

"Oops," Amy said, shaking her head and laughing. "Looks like we better start calling her Frederika from now on."

Carter frowned, running fingers through his hair so that it stood up like an animal pelt. "Just exactly how did this happen?" he said. "When did you get Fred, anyway?"

Scamp thought hard. "Las' week," he said at last.

Carter and Amy looked at each other and grinned. "Okay," Carter allowed. "I thought he was a beloved family pet, and here he was fresh off the pet store shelf."

"'Beloved' is a relative term," Amy told him, laughing.

Distracted as she was, it wasn't difficult to get the little mouse back into the cage with all her babies around her. And somehow that seemed to put to rest any feelings of unease that were lingering with the children. Fred was back in the cage and all was right with the world. Almost.

"I wish Mommy would come home," Scamp said as he watched the mother and babies interact.

Amy dropped down to hug him. "She will, darling. It won't be long now. You'll have her back, good as new, and your daddy, too."

He hugged her back, breaking out a warm spot in her heart she'd been saving just for him.

* * *

And then a terrible thing happened. The Joliet Aire people came a day early.

It started out like any other day, full of disasters. Scamp dropped a carton of milk on the kitchen floor. It burst open and milk seeped everywhere, into every tiny crack, every opening it could find. Amy knew only a full soaking would flush out all risk of the room taking on a permanent sour smell and she immediately got to work on it.

Meanwhile, Carter lost an important file when his computer locked up. She had to close the door to the den to keep the tender young ears from hearing a lot of hard swearing. She went outside to hook up the hose for washing down the kitchen, attaching the pressure nozzle, and the children went out with her, but Deedee immediately got stung by a bee so she rushed back into the bathroom with the shrieking child. The baby began crying, as well, and she called to Carter to take care of Jillian while she comforted Deedee.

Chaos. She realized that if all this had happened during her first week here, she might have been reduced to quiet sobbing in a corner somewhere. But now she felt she could handle it. Having Carter helped, of course, but more than that had changed. *She* had. She still wanted to tear out her hair, but she didn't feel the temptation to call 9-1-1.

Just as she was congratulating herself on having grown, she realized there was a lot of commotion in the front yard. And then Scamp came running into the house, calling out, "I didn't mean to!"

"Oh, no," Amy moaned as she grabbed Deedee in her arms and headed for the front porch to see what was going on.

Yanking open the door, she found the walkway littered with three Frenchmen who had probably arrived impeccably dressed in fine European suits. Now they were soaked to the skin and angry as scalded cats. Obviously, Scamp had gotten a little wild with the hose.

"I just put it down and it did it by itself," Scamp cried, close to tears.

Her first impulse was to close the door and run for the hills. Maybe Monsieur Jobert hadn't recognized her. But no, he was already yelling her name. Too late for any sort of escape.

It took some time and all the French she knew to calm them down. She worked hard at mollifying them, all the while silently cursing whoever had given out the address where she and Carter could be found. She knew they made a strange picture, she with a tear-stained Deedee in her arms, and Carter, when he joined them, with a baby on his hip. Scamp was hiding under the bed, but once he could be cajoled back out, he apologized to the men. That and a taste of an exquisite omelet quickly whipped up by Carter seemed to tame the troubled spirits of the French.

"All in all, that was very unprofessional," she noted to Carter after their visitors had left.

"Undoubtedly," Carter agreed. "But I think once we got down to talking about the issue at hand, things went rather smoothly."

They had made plans to meet at TriTerraCorp headquarters the next day for the full presentation. Amy contacted Cheryl Park, the neighbor who often baby-sat for the children and had her come early in the morning. She hadn't wanted to do it, but one day wouldn't be so bad, especially now that the children had settled down and understood that nothing terrible was happening to their parents, and that they would be seeing them soon.

It felt good to be dressing for work right at daybreak. Almost like the old days.

"Except that I'm not the old me," she told herself in the mirror.

She and Carter drove together to the office, staking out a conference room and preparing the slides and overhead projection panels, quizzing each other nervously from time to time, greeting old friends and trying to stay focused.

They'd gathered in a few other employees to help with different aspect of the proposal. Chareen Wolf was one. A paralegal experienced in contract negotiations, Carter had asked her to bone up on French real estate law. She was to cover some of the more technical legal ramifications. Considering that she was about to marry one of the newest vice presidents, Michael Greco, in just a few days, they were extremely grateful that she could take the time.

"I'd give up my honeymoon to score this one," Chareen told them with a grin. "If we can pull this off, we'll be the talk of the development industry."

And then it was time. Show time.

All in all, they both felt the presentation went very well. Mr. Jobert was noncomittal, but at least he wasn't scathing.

"At least," Carter said that evening back at the den in the house, as they both ate from Chinese take-out cartons and went back over every minute detail of the day. "At least he didn't laugh."

He didn't laugh. In fact, Amy was pretty sure he was impressed.

The next day Carter drove the French delegation up to visit the Black Stones Beach Resort just south of Carmel, and the White Stones project that was currently under development closer to home. Both had been TriTerraCorp jobs and both were bound to impress the Europeans. Amy stayed home chewing her nails and waiting to hear. She knew the visitors were leaving the next afternoon, so surely they would know the verdict very soon. She only hoped the decision was a good one. It would mean so much to Carter.

He got home late and he was very tired, but he was pretty pleased with the way things had gone.

"They were blown away by White Stones," he

said. "Who wouldn't be? It's state-of-the-art for resorts. They won't find a better company to work with. I only hope they realize that."

"Well, we'll know by tomorrow afternoon."

He nodded. "Their flight is at three. We'll know by then."

The next day seemed to drag interminably. Amy looked at the clock every two minutes and the hands never seemed to move. By eleven, when no call had come to meet the Frenchmen at the office, they began to feel apprehensive. Every little noise the young ones made caused them to grit their teeth to keep from yelling at them. By twelve, they had sent the children out to play in the yard and were pacing the floor.

"Call, call, call," Amy chanted softly, staring at the telephone.

Carter merely growled.

"You don't suppose they would leave without saying what their decision was?" she cried, horrified by the thought.

Carter didn't answer. His face was beginning to look haggard.

A thump came from the front yard. Amy rose, listening. Then a cry. It was Scamp's voice, and the cry was strangely strangled. Her heart in her throat, she ran for the front door.

He wasn't on the porch. She ran to the steps, and then she saw him. He'd been climbing on the railing again and had fallen, just as she'd warned him he would a thousand times.

"Oh, Scamp," she cried, rushing to him. And then she saw the blood.

"Scamp!" She tried to keep her panic out of her voice, but it wasn't easy. He had his hands in front of his mouth and there was blood spilling between his fingers, making it very difficult to see just exactly what had happened. "Carter!"

He was there right away, lifting Scamp and carrying him into the house. The poor boy was whimpering, and when he saw the blood on his own hands, he gasped and turned pale, turning his huge eyes toward Carter and then toward Amy in a silent plea to make it all okay.

"Don't worry, honey," Amy told him, fighting to stay calm. "We're going to take care of this. Let me wash it a little…"

Carter held him up at the kitchen sink and she tried dabbing at his mouth with a wet cloth but he cried out and pulled away when she did so. It was then that she saw that his teeth had broken all the way through his lower lip about halfway down to his chin, and were sticking through the other side. A wave of horrified nausea hit her, but she fought it back.

"We've got to get him to the emergency room," she told Carter, and he nodded, agreeing with her.

"Can you hold him here at the sink?" he said, cool and steady. "I'll get the car."

She nodded, taking over while Carter started toward the garage.

And that was when the telephone rang.

They both looked at it and looked at each other. Carter reached for the receiver. "Hello?"

He nodded to Amy, letting her know it was the call they had been expecting. The Frenchman spoke perfect English, informing him that Monsieur Jobert had an announcement to make and would like the two of them to meet him at the office immediately.

Carter didn't hesitate. "Look, I can't come," he said. "I've got an emergency going on."

Amy gasped, and Carter held the phone enough away from his ear so that she could hear the reaction along with him.

"Monsieur Jobert is getting on the plane in one hour," the man on the phone said acerbically. "You must come right now or the entire deal is off."

Amy looked at him, feeling frantic. "You've got to go see him," she said, her arm around Scamp, who was whimpering softly. "I can...I can handle this. I can drive and..."

Carter shook his head. "No, you can't do it alone. You need my help. And I want to be there with you, anyway." Into the telephone, he said, "Monsieur Jobert will have to wait. And if he can't wait, perhaps I can come to see him in Paris. But right now, I have a family emergency that can't be postponed. I'm sorry, but I cannot come to see him. Goodbye."

Hanging up, he raced outside to get the car. Amy watched him go, her heart sinking.

It was only later that Amy fully realized just what Carter had done. Later, after the whole lot of them had gone storming into the emergency room with Scamp, after the nurse had cleaned him up and the doctor had pulled his lip back where it belonged and put in the necessary stitches. Later, after she'd held Deedee in the waiting room and watched Carter pace around the place with baby Jillian in his arms.

That was when she realized that he had given up a business opportunity—heck, more than an opportunity, a gold mine—to take care of human needs instead. He'd broken his own rule and put a relationship and compassion ahead of success. And she only loved him all the more for it.

It wasn't as if the Joliet Aire project was a lost cause. Carter already had a reservation for a flight to Paris. He would go, hat in hand, and Monsieur Jobert would probably give him the contract. But for now, she was glad he'd done what he did. Maybe he was changing, just like she was.

Scamp was fine. They said he'd always have a scar on his lower lip, but by now he'd decided that was going to be cool.

While they were hanging around the hospital, Carter managed to talk a floor nurse into letting him take Deedee and Jillian in to see Meg for just a moment, even though the rules didn't allow children under ten. For that, Amy knew, Meg would be forever grateful.

"That will change her mind about him," she told herself smugly.

Carter was a great guy and she wanted everyone to know it. She only wished…well, she wished a lot of things. Still, what she already had was pretty darn good, and maybe she ought to just be a little grateful herself.

They got home late, tired and hungry, and Amy fixed dinner for them all, a quick dish of spaghetti sauce on angel hair pasta that even Carter pronounced pretty good. Scamp didn't get to eat; he was too sleepy from the medication he'd received and had gone straight to bed. Deedee and Jillian followed soon after, and Amy was alone with Carter for the first time all day.

When she came down from the children's room, she found him sitting on the couch, staring into space. Quietly, she slipped in beside him.

"You did a good thing today," she said softly.

He turned and looked down at her. "Good, or stupid?" he asked.

"Good," she said firmly. "No doubt in my mind."

He looked at the way her eyes were shining and he almost believed her. "We'll see," he said, but his mind was losing its business focus. She was so close and she smelled so good, she was filling his head with dangerous ideas. Leaning close, he nuzzled a kiss into the soft spot behind her ear and then he tasted her skin with his tongue.

She sighed and for once she didn't push him away immediately. Instead she let her head fall back and closed her eyes, and that was all the invitation he needed. He kissed her, gathering her up in his arms at the same time, as though he would carry her to heaven if she let him. He held her close. She tasted like rose petals and felt like silk. His body reacted so quickly and so strongly that he groaned out loud, his need for her as sudden and urgent as a thunderstorm.

She seemed to feel it, too, moving in his arms like quicksilver, taking as much from his mouth as he was taking from hers. She was light and sound, softness and the cutting edge. She was a goddess too sacred to touch and a woman, hot and moist and hungry for him. She was every woman he had ever known and more of a woman than any he'd ever thought could exist.

He wanted her so badly, he felt he could have broken any commandment, challenged any rival, torn apart stone walls with his bare hands just to have her. And yet, when she stirred, opening her eyes, and put a hand on his shoulder and said, "Carter...please..." he stopped. It wasn't easy. Reining in the fire that had been ignited was painful and frustrating, but he did it. For her. Because at the moment, he would have done anything for her.

Her eyes were clear and full of an affection he

could have died for. "I love you," she said softly.
And then she was up and off the couch and out of
the room and he knew he wasn't going to see her
again until morning.

Chapter Ten

Meg and Tim would be coming home soon—Meg sooner than Tim. In a few days this idyllic situation would come to an end. Things were winding down and Amy was beginning to realize how much she was going to miss it.

Facts were facts. She was madly in love with Carter. There was no getting around it. There was no wiggle room. She was deeply, fully and thoroughly in love with him. And she knew it was hopeless. He had no more interest in marriage than he did in joining a spelunking team. She would not be spending the rest of her life with him. It just wasn't in the cards.

But she wanted what was best for him and she wanted him to be happy. And that was why she contacted Delia and asked her to help in finding Carter's sister, Callie. Delia obliged very quickly, and came back with a telephone number. Amy called it.

"Hi," she said when Callie James Anderson answered the phone. "I am...or rather, I have been your brother Carter's administrative associate for the last two years. I'll be honest with you. I care for him very much. I want to see him happy. He's told me something about the background in your family and I'd like to find a way to get you all together again."

"Well, aren't you a sweetheart." Callie seemed a warm and genuine woman.

"I just think it's important for him to connect with his family again."

"Believe me, I've wanted the same thing for years now. He's been so elusive. We have a family reunion every year. In fact, it's coming up next month in Santa Barbara. He's never come."

"Never?"

"No. And I always make sure he gets an invitation. But he refuses. I don't know why. Sometimes I wonder if he knows why. But he won't come."

Amy sighed. "I'm going to do anything I can to get him to come this year."

"Bless you. And please, you come, too. In fact, I hope you come whether or not he does. We'd love to meet you."

"You know, I think I would like that, too."

"Good. Please do come. I'll send you the information."

Amy hung up and stared out the window. Somehow, she was going to get him to go to his family reunion. Some deep instinct told her it was important that he go. That it just might save his life.

"Well, that's a bit dramatic, I suppose," she said when she tried to explain how she felt to him, as she was telling him about the reunion. "But I really think you need to connect with your family again. To be whole."

"Psychobabble," he said dismissively. "I've got better things to do."

She'd given him all the information. She only hoped that he would look at it. "I'm going," she said, holding his gaze with her own. "Go with me."

He pulled his gaze away and scoffed. "I don't want to go, Amy. If you want to go, fine. But don't try to drag me into it."

He wouldn't discuss it any further. She was baffled by his attitude and angry at herself for having presented the whole thing wrong. But there wasn't much time to work on him. He was leaving for Paris, and while he was gone, Meg would be coming home. That meant they would never be together this way again. That knowledge made her ache inside, but once again, facts were facts.

Just knowing her time here was almost up made her appreciate every moment with the children in a way she never had before, and that night, she felt especially loving to dark-haired Deedee as she put her into her toddler bed and tucked the covers in around her.

Suddenly Deedee threw her little arms around Amy's neck and hugged tight. "Ni'nite," she said. "Lub you."

"Night, night, sweetheart," Amy said emotionally, giving her a kiss on her dear pink cheek. "I love you, too. More than anything."

Her heart was suddenly full. There was nothing more wonderful than the spontaneous affection of a child. And when she got to the hallway, she let her tears flow and cried for all that had happened here, all that had gone wrong, all that had gone right, all that was yet to be.

And then she dried her tears and went down to face Carter. It was time they got things settled between them. She dreaded it, and yet she knew once it was all out in the open, she could begin to get on with her life.

"This is it. You're leaving for Paris in the morning. And when you get back, Meg will be home."

He nodded.

They sat side by side and neither said a word for a long time. Finally, Carter turned and looked into her eyes.

"I'd like you to come back to work for me, Amy. I need you. I can't be the best that I can be without you. So I'm asking you, straight out. Please come back."

She started to speak and he touched her lips with his forefinger, stopping her.

"Let me say one more thing. We've both revealed

a lot about ourselves over the past few weeks. I think you know me about as well as anyone ever has. But I just want to explain something again.''

He looked away, taking a deep breath. ''When I started out in business, I was good at it right from the beginning. I had a lot of success, a lot of good feedback. Gaining confidence, I became the person I am today.''

He looked back into her eyes. ''All the things that got torn away from me by people I loved—well, I felt I sort of restored that through my success in business. Business became everything to me.'' His eyes darkened. ''And I thought you were sort of the same way. That you needed business the way I did. We were such a team.''

He shook his head and she waited, knowing he had more to say.

''I really couldn't understand why you thought you needed more than that. And I still think you will find that business will give you more satisfaction than anything else. I'd like you to think seriously about that. And I hope when you do, you'll come back to work.''

She waited a moment to be sure he didn't have any more to say, then she shook her head, holding back tears. ''I'm going to stay with Meg for the time being,'' she said. ''And then look for another job.''

He winced. ''You won't come back to work?'' He hesitated, then added, ''Even part-time?''

''No.'' Reaching out, she put the palm of her

hand against his cheek. "I'm sorry. I have to move on with my life. I love my work and I'd love to keep my hand in but I have to turn my back on it for a while. I have to put as much into establishing a family as I did into establishing a career. I'm going to have to concentrate on it full-time. Because I don't really have much time."

She saw the pain in his eyes and she felt her tears begin to spill over.

"So, no, Carter, I won't be coming back to work." She took a shaky breath. "I'm going to stay with Meg until she gets completely back on her feet again, help her out with the children until she's strong enough to take that over. And then...I'll be looking for a husband."

He grabbed her hand and planted a kiss in the center of her palm. "Amy, you know how I feel about that. I can't offer you a husband. I can offer you a lover. But not a husband."

She nodded, blinking back her tears. "That's not enough for me."

"I know that." Softly, he kissed her lips. "Good luck," he said, his voice husky. And then he rose and left the room.

Carter left for Paris the next morning and that afternoon, the workmen were back, breaking down all the changes in the den and restoring it to the quiet room it had been before Carter moved in. As each piece of office equipment was packed up and moved out, Amy felt a piece of her happiness leave with it.

There were times when she wondered if she were making a big mistake. After all, how often did you find a man to love like Carter James? He would never marry her, but she could work with him for years, sharing a life and a love and the work they both thrived on. What more could she ask for, really? Most people never even got that much.

But if she chose that road, she knew she would never have children, never have marriage, never have the sort of life that seemed good and natural to her at some fundamental level she just couldn't shake. And despite all the ups and downs with the kids, she'd learned to love them almost as much as she loved Carter, and she knew she would never be happy knowing she had voluntarily given up her chance at having children of her own.

No, she couldn't do that. Family and a sense of belonging to something lasting were just too important to her. She couldn't turn her back on elements that made her the person she was.

Meg came home, at last. Amy and the children worked all the day before, cleaning and fixing flower arrangements and printing up a huge Welcome Home banner to display over the doorway. It was touching to watch her reunion with her children. Amy cried and hoped with all her heart that someday she would have little ones who loved her just as much as these kids loved her sister.

Meg's legs were still in casts and she couldn't get around without help. Tim would be coming home in a few days. Once he was there, they had hired a part-time nurse to help with things and Amy would begin to withdraw her support little by little. Meanwhile, she was happy to do everything she could to help her sister.

Carter called her from the office when he returned from Paris. Monsieur Jobert had been disappointed that she hadn't made the trip, but he had okayed the contract and the legal people were working out the details. He told her that the two of them were in line for a very generous bonus.

"You'll have a nice cushion to keep you from starving while you go looking for a husband," he told her dryly.

"Good," she said, refusing to rise to his bait.

He asked about the children and hesitated when she suggested he come over and visit. But he turned her down. And she knew he was right to. There was no point in prolonging the inevitable.

She said goodbye and sat down, waiting for the tears to come. But nothing happened. This time, her sorrow was too deep for tears.

By the time the family reunion rolled around, Amy had moved back into her own place and was settling down to looking for a new job. She thought about skipping the James family party, but at the last minute, her curiosity wouldn't let her stay away. She wanted to see what Carter's family members looked like.

And she found out they looked pretty darn good. The family resemblance was downright eerie. There was Callie, in her early thirties, married with two children and a very nice husband. She looked like a female version of Carter, and Amy loved her at first sight.

Then there was Ben, in his late twenties, lighter and skinnier, and very funny; Gloria, twenty-five and gorgeous, trying for a film career; Jimmy, twenty-three, just graduating from law school: Libby, still in college. Meeting them all and listening to their happy chatter made her long for Carter to see this. She knew he would be proud of them. Proud and very happy to know they had all turned out so well.

They had games and snacks and drinks with umbrellas in them and then there was meat grilling on the barbecue. One of the younger boys brought out a guitar and played for everyone. One of the younger girls sang. And then it was time to eat.

The food was great, though Amy kept thinking Carter could have added a bit of pizzazz to some of the recipes if he'd been involved. No one asked her why he wasn't attending. Everyone knew he just didn't want to be involved, and she could see it hurt them, though few commented.

Callie did tell her that they had all decided they wanted to find some way to tell Carter how much they appreciated all he'd done for them when they were young and he'd held the family together for as long as possible.

"We had a little speech prepared, just in case he showed up," she told her.

"Maybe next year," Amy said.

If only, she kept thinking. *If only.*

And suddenly her heart stopped. There he was, walking into the backyard, looking very cool and very wary. His gaze was searching until it met hers, and then something changed in his eyes and she started toward him, drawn almost magnetically.

But before she got to him, everyone had noticed and they were all crowding around him. He was being introduced to each and every one of them, and little by little, his face began to lose its wary look.

Just relax, she told him silently, echoing the very thing he'd told her when she'd been so stiff around the children. And he seemed to hear the message, because he was doing just that.

Her heart was thumping in her chest when he finally turned to her, his eyes warm. They came together as though they just couldn't help themselves. She lifted up onto her toes, slipping her arms around his neck, and he brought her in close and kissed her as though he would never stop.

She clung to him. "Oh, Carter," she whispered.

"Amy, Amy, I've missed you so much," he whispered back.

They pulled apart to look at each other and Amy noticed that the others had melted away to another part of the yard to play volleyball, and she thanked Callie silently. She'd told Callie all about the situation between her and Carter, and Callie would know enough to give them a bit of privacy.

"I'm so glad you came to see your family," she said. "Carter, I know it was hard for you to come. I think you're wonderful."

"I figured, if you cared enough to come when you aren't even related to these people, it was the least I could do." His blue eyes took her in as though he couldn't get enough of her. "But I can't believe you actually came." He shook his head, searching her eyes. "Why, Amy?"

She smiled. It was simple. "Because I love you," she said.

He stared at her for a long moment, then swore softly. "I'm such a fool," he said.

She nodded. "I'll second that emotion," she told him. "But you're still the man I love, so I guess I could learn to put up with it."

He frowned, unsure. "What are you saying?"

She laid her hand against his chest and gazed at him earnestly. "Carter, I've told you I love you a number of times now. It's only polite to reciprocate."

"I..." He hesitated, looking to the side as though searching for an escape hatch.

"Come on," she coaxed, touching his cheek lovingly. "You can do it if you try."

He looked back down at her. "Amy, I will tell you this. You know how I told you that business was everything to me. That I thought it was all I needed?"

She nodded.

"Well, that is the way it's always been. But..." He swallowed hard. "I found out it wasn't that way anymore. I finally realized that business was only enough for me...when you were there."

Her smile was serene. She knew she was going to get what she wanted. It was just a matter of time. "And?" she said, urging him on. "What does that lead you to believe?"

He groaned. "Oh hell, Amy. You know I love you."

"I know it. I'm just not convinced you know it yet."

"What will it take to convince you?"

"A marriage proposal."

"Okay. You've got one."

"I do? Where is it?"

"You mean, you actually want me to go through the whole rigmarole?"

"Absolutely."

"Okay. Here goes." He cleared his throat and

took both of her hands in his. "Amy Pendleton, will you marry me?"

She smiled up at him, her face shining with happiness. "Carter James, I will marry you."

He took a shaky breath. "My God. That means..."

"We're going to get married."

He winced. "I always swore I'd never do that."

She grinned. "That'll teach you not to swear." She shivered. Happiness like this was so good it was almost scary. She took his arm. "Shall we go tell your family?"

He nodded, looking a little stunned. "I only came to say hello," he said. "I'm not sure how I ended up engaged to be married."

She laughed. "Don't worry about it. I'll handle everything." She smiled up at him. "And next year, the reunion can be at our house."

* * * * *

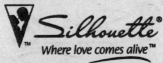

**Where royalty and romance
go hand in hand...**

The series continues in Silhouette Romance
with these unforgettable novels:

HER ROYAL HUSBAND
by Cara Colter
on sale July 2002 (SR #1600)

THE PRINCESS HAS AMNESIA!
by Patricia Thayer
on sale August 2002 (SR #1606)

SEARCHING FOR HER PRINCE
by Karen Rose Smith
on sale September 2002 (SR #1612)

And look for more Crown and Glory stories in
SILHOUETTE DESIRE starting in October 2002!

Available at your favorite retail outlet.

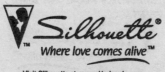

Where love comes alive™

eHARLEQUIN.com

community | membership

buy books | authors | online reads | magazine | learn to write

buy books

Your one-stop shop for great reads at great prices. We have all your favorite Harlequin, Silhouette, MIRA and Steeple Hill books, as well as a host of other bestsellers in Other Romances. Discover a wide array of new releases, bargains and hard-to-find books today!

learn to write

Become the writer you always knew you could be: get tips and tools on how to craft the perfect romance novel and have your work critiqued by professional experts in romance fiction. Follow your dream now!

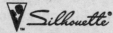

Silhouette®

Where love comes alive™—online...

Where Texas society reigns supreme—and appearances are *everything*.

Coming in June 2002
Stroke of Fortune by Christine Rimmer

Millionaire rancher and eligible bachelor Flynt Carson struck a hole in one when his Sunday golf ritual at the Lone Star Country Club unveiled an abandoned baby girl. Flynt felt he had no business raising a child, and desperately needed the help of former flame Josie Lavender. Though this woman was too innocent for his tarnished soul, the love-struck nanny was determined to help him raise the mysterious baby—and what happened next was anyone's guess!

Available at your favorite retail outlet.

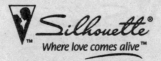

Start Your Summer With Sizzle
And Silhouette Books!

In June 2002, look for these HOT volumes led by
New York Times bestselling authors and
receive a free Gourmet Garden kit!

Retail value of $17.00 U.S.

THE BLUEST EYES IN TEXAS by Joan Johnston
and **WIFE IN NAME ONLY** by Carolyn Zane

THE LEOPARD'S WOMAN by Linda Lael Miller
and **WHITE WOLF** by Lindsay McKenna

THE BOUNTY by Rebecca Brandewyne
and **A LITTLE TEXAS TWO-STEP** by Peggy Moreland

OVERLOAD by Linda Howard
and **IF A MAN ANSWERS** by Merline Lovelace

**This exciting promotion is available at your
favorite retail outlet. See inside books for details.**

Only from

Silhouette®
Where love comes alive™

Visit Silhouette at www.eHarlequin.com   PSNCP02

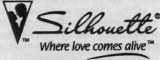

COMING NEXT MONTH